"Do you think you could convincingly fight with me?"

Carrie folded her arms across her chest. "Without the slightest bit of trouble."

"Terrific." James smiled down at her, his eyes going silvery. "First I think I should kiss you again."

Her heart thudded, and her breathing was ragged. "You mean you kiss me and I struggle with you?" She swallowed hard.

"No, no. First we have a long, intense embrace, and then we have our fight. And this time try to act as though you're enjoying it."

"Why, you—"

Laughing, he brushed the words right off her lips, his mouth so tender that she thought she might swoon. "I can't win with you, my darling, can I?" he whispered against her lips.

Jennifer Rose *loves to travel in search of material for her books, but she is happiest in New York City, where she lives with her husband and children. She spends her spare time playing word and board games, arranging flowers, seeking gastronomic rareties, and taking walks without destination.*

Dear Reader:

The lazy days of summer are here, a perfect time to enjoy July's SECOND CHANCE AT LOVE romances.

In *Master Touch* (#274) Jasmine Craig reintroduces Hollywood idol Damion Tanner, who you'll remember as Lynn Frampton's boss in *Dear Adam* (#243). Damion *looks* like a typical devastating womanizer, but inside he's a man of intriguing depth, complexity, and contradictory impulses. He dislikes Alessandra Hawkins on sight, but can't resist pursuing her. Alessandra is thoroughly disdainful of Damion, and equally smitten. You'll love reading how these two marvelously antagonistic characters walk backward into love — resisting all the way!

In *Night of a Thousand Stars* (#275) Petra Diamond takes you where no couple has gone before — to sex in space! Astronaut Jennie Jacobs and ace pilot Dean Bradshaw have *all* the "right stuff" for such an experiment, but they've had little time to explore their more tender feelings. Suddenly their emotions catch up with them, making their coming together a bristly, challenging proposition. Petra Diamond handles their love story with sensitive realism, making *Night of a Thousand Stars* out of this world.

Laine Allen, an exciting newcomer, turns romance stereotypes on their heads in *Undercover Kisses* (#276). Every time private eye Katrina Langley asks herself, "How wrong could a woman be about a man," ultra-manly Moss Adams suggests the answer: "Very wrong!" Every time Kat thinks they're evenly matched, Moss cheerfully knocks her off balance. Moss's intelligent deviltry and Kat's swift-witted ripostes will keep you chuckling as you discover the secrets they keep from each other, while unraveling a most perplexing intrigue.

SECOND CHANCE AT LOVE is pleased to introduce another new writer — Elizabeth Henry, author of *Man Trouble* (#277). Like other heroines you've met, Marcy has a low opinion of men — especially Rick Davenport, who climbs through her bedroom window after midnight and challenges her to all sorts of fun and games. But no other heroine must contend with an alter ego called Nosy, who butts in with unasked-for advice. Nonstop banter makes *Man Trouble* as light, crunchy, and fun to consume as popcorn.

In *Suddenly That Summer* (#278) by Jennifer Rose, Carrie Delaney's so fed up with the dating game that she spends a week at a tacky singles resort, determined to find a husband. But she's so busy participating in the toga party, forest scavenger hunt, and after-dark skinny dip that she refuses to recognize the man of her dreams — even when he insists he's "it"! Thank goodness James Luddington has the cleverness and persistence to win Carrie by fair means or foul. Finding a mate has never been so confusing — or so much fun!

In *Sweet Enchantment* (#279), Diana Mars employs warmth and skill to convey the joys and heartaches of combining two families into one through a new marriage. Pamela Shaw, whom you know as Barrett Shaw's sister-in-law in *Sweet Trespass* (#182), has to deal with her son's antagonism toward her new love, Grady Talliver, *and* with Grady's four young sons. But lizards in the bathroom, a bed sprayed with perfume, and a chamber of horrors in the attic don't ruffle our heroine, who more than adequately turns the tables on her little darlings. *Sweet Enchantment* is a story many of you will identify with — and all of you will enjoy.

Have fun!

Ellen Edwards

Ellen Edwards, Senior Editor
SECOND CHANCE AT LOVE
The Berkley Publishing Group
200 Madison Avenue
New York, N.Y. 10016

Second Chance at Love®

SUDDENLY THAT SUMMER

JENNIFER ROSE

A
SECOND CHANCE AT LOVE
BOOK

Second Chance at Love books are published by
The Berkley Publishing Group
200 Madison Avenue, New York, NY 10016

For Bob, who gave me Alt-T;
and for Rose and Albert,
who gave me time to use it.

All or Nothing

O Love, destroy all power to love
or grant all lovers their deserving;
blot out desire from wretched hearts
or let its fire kindle a mutual fire.

—Lucillius
(First Century Greek)

Author's Note

Suddenly That Summer is my eighth and last category romance. Eight! Some romance writers don't really begin counting until they get into double digits, but since I meant to write only one, I feel like someone who reaches into a half-pound box of chocolates for a single luscious piece only to discover a few minutes later that the entire contents of the box has mysteriously disappeared.

My first romance, *Out of a Dream*, was number four in the Second Chance at Love line. I wrote it without having seen any other books in the line—indeed, after having read a grand total of two category romances, both by Charlotte Lamb—mostly because I had always planned to write one novel for every type of genre. Reading it in print was satisfying (I cried over the last page), and I liked the Second Chance idea and the people connected with the line, and I was a single mother with a lot of second-chance fantasies to work out, so I decided to write one more. And the nougat-filled chocolate turned out to be as luscious as the caramel center, and after that I wrote "just one more."

Then a lovely thing happened. I married again and

got my own real-life second chance. I'm not at all sure it's mere coincidence that my husband looks like Matt from *Out of a Dream*, talks like George from *Shamrock Season*, and kisses like Doug from *Twilight Embrace*.

No sooner had we exchanged our vows than Jove decided to bring out a series of romances about married love: To Have and to Hold. I wrote one of the launch books, *A Taste of Heaven*, and by then I was hooked on the romance genre. I wrote four more novels for Second Chance and To Have and to Hold, telling myself that each one was the last. Now—because eight is my favorite number, therefore a good stopping place—I really have to get on with my ambition to write one of every genre. Another piece of this gorgeous chocolate called romance, and I will never eat a bean sprout again.

I've had the good luck to know some wonderful, talented people in the romance field. My thanks to three terrific editors, Beverly Lewis, Carolyn Nichols, and, especially, Ellen Edwards; and to Jane Rotrosen and Andrea Cirillo, my agents. A kiss to Victor Temkin, who got me to Jove in the first place.

Special thanks also go to my sister-in-law Katharine Weber, a talented essayist, who has been known to buy my books by the half dozen at her local pharmacy and leave copies in friends' cars in the parking lot; to Kay Swift, the composer and song-writer, who has been an unfailing source of romantic inspiration, and at least one of her songs has figured in the plot of all eight books; and to my parents, who have indulgently read every word of each romance (well, maybe they've skimmed the love scenes).

For their help with *Suddenly That Summer,* I am grateful to Nicki Holtzman and her family, who suggested a Sugarbush vacation; to Jim Wyllie, creator of the IBM Personal Editor program; and to Sharifa Hamid, who kept my baby son from eating my research materials and who always had an encouraging word to say about my romances.

"Don't say good-bye," my husband advises from over my shoulder. "You may want to come back." I know what he means. It's hard to imagine never writing another romance. We were in Hawaii last month; can I resist creating a love scene in which the hero and heroine get Maui potato-chip crumbs in bed? But as readers who can't resist "just one more," I'm sure you sympathize with writers who have the same problem, so please don't laugh if my adieu turns out to be au revoir. In any event, may all your dreams come true—and thanks for letting me into your hearts.

SUDDENLY
THAT SUMMER

CHAPTER ONE

"MY FELLOW GUESTS at The Ladders, I'm pleased to announce that one lucky man among you will win a fabulous door prize before the week is out— marriage to the brilliant, the beautiful, the altogether delicious and desirable Carrie Delaney!"

Giving a sultry toss to her dark hair and tugging suggestively at the belt of her pale green robe, Carrie grinned at her reflection in the fluorescent-lit bathroom mirror and vamped for all she was worth.

"Yes, the event that the men of America have been waiting for has finally arrived," she went on giddily as she added a coat of mascara to the long lashes framing her large hazel eyes. "The afore-mentioned Widow Delaney, having mourned for a year and dated for two, has finally decided that the

1

time has come to make a New Life for herself and her darling daughter." Dropping her mascara wand into her daisy-pattern cosmetic bag, she added in the low, wry tones of her normal voice, "Because the single life stinks."

Her zany monologue was interrupted by the sound of a tornado striking the adjoining bedroom: six-year-old Dannie, on a tour of their rented chalet, bursting open the door and jumping onto Carrie's beige chenille-covered double bed.

"This is a much better trampoline than my bed," the slender child exclaimed, her long dark hair wafting as she flew up and down, making the springs squeak crazily. "Want to trade with me?"

"Dannie Delaney, how many times have I told you to knock on other people's doors before entering?"

A hurt expression crossed Dannie's elfin face, and her jumping slowed down to a mere bounce. "You're not other people, you're my mother."

Swallowing an exasperated sigh, Carrie gathered Dannie up and held her close. Just what she needed to smooth the path of romance—a bed with tattle-tale springs and a daughter who believed that doors had been invented for the fun of kicking them open.

On the other hand, what was as important as the incredibly intimate bond between Dannie and herself? On the other, other hand, the best way she could show her love for Dannie was by finding the girl a new father. And a grown-ups-only bedroom (with discreet springs) wouldn't hurt the cause.

Murmuring reassuring words, Carrie plunked Dannie down in front of the walk-in closet and asked her to help choose a dress for that evening.

Mondays at The Ladders featured what the brochure had called Our Festive Cocktail Mixer—Enjoy A Refreshing Mixed Drink Gratis While Mixing With New Friends. Carrie was an English teacher, and the coy proliferation of capital letters set her teeth on edge. But never mind. She was here, and she was going to make the most of it, and then, if fate were kind, she could forget about Mixing for the next fifty years or so.

A half-hour later, dressed in the yellow and white striped French cotton dress Dannie had picked out, Carrie kissed her daughter good night and gave instructions about bedtime to the sitter, a plump and placid sixteen-year-old named Gretchen Smith, who'd been highly recommended by the assistant manager of The Ladders. Closing the door to the two-bedroom chalet called Zermatt, Carrie stepped out onto the wooden walkway, smiled up at the soft, dark pine trees, and took a deep breath of the fragrant Vermont air.

It was a betwixt-and-between time of day, later than afternoon and earlier than evening, and a betwixt-and-between time of year, the third week in August, technically still summer but beginning to feel like fall. Well, she fit right in, Carrie told herself wryly, heading down the ladderlike steps that gave the resort its name. She was no longer Gar Delaney's wife, and she wasn't quite yet Mrs. Somebody Else.

After her firefighter husband had died in a heroic rescue attempt, she had mourned for a full year—less out of respect for custom than in obedience to the state of her heart. Then her mother and sisters and friends, even Gar's parents and his chief, had conspired to drag her back into the wild world of men.

Over and over again she'd had to hear the impertinent phrases: "Gar would want you to be happy." "Gar would want you to marry again." And always: "You owe it to Dannie."

There was no denying that Dannie pined for family life. Put three string beans on her plate, and they were Mama, Papa, and Girl. But where, oh, where was the man who was worthy of Dannie, whose picture deserved to share space on her dresser with the portrait of Gar in its heart-shaped frame?

Carrie had seemed to have a genius for attracting men who were interested in sex, money, trendy restaurants, sports, and more sex—and only incidentally in that most adorable of little girls, Danielle McGrath Delaney. They'd showed up with teddy bears, Lego blocks, and glossy picture books in hopes of getting Mommy to let down her guard and share her narrow bed.

She'd read a dozen magazine articles about the horde of single fathers out there, but they hadn't been the ones who'd offered her drinks in bars or asked her how to pick ripe cantaloupes in grocery stores. She'd haunted the Central Park Zoo on Saturday mornings and the Museum of Natural History on Sundays, bravely striking up conversations with likely-looking men while Dannie glutted herself on monkeys and dinosaurs. But all those cute blue-jeaned, sneakered guys with kids in backpacks had turned out to have wives at home. Of course, if she wanted to have an affair, many of them were ready to oblige.

She'd grown to detest the opening lines of men on the make, the sizing-up of intimate flesh, all the sad and seamy rituals of the mating game. She'd felt as if she'd been condemned to live adolescence twice—and once had been more than enough.

But Dannie needed that new father, and—face it, Delaney—she herself needed love. She couldn't go on talking aloud in the shower and pretending it was conversation. She could no longer trick herself out of loneliness with the oh-so-single Japanese futon she'd bought to sleep on when she and Dannie had moved from the Gar-haunted Upper West Side down to Greenwich Village.

Wretchedly unfair though it was, Gar was permanently dead. And she was very much alive.

So on she'd plowed, developing a list of class-A baby-sitters, becoming expert at applying blusher to her cheekbones, learning to weed out in a hurry the respectable-looking Wall Street lawyers who had an after-hours interest in blackjack or heavy drinking. Naturally a hopeful soul, she'd felt flutter after flutter of possibility—especially when a dashing sociology professor had moved into her building, crayon drawings prominent among his possessions. But although he'd proved to be a sweet daddy on weekends, she'd discovered that his week nights were dedicated to giving "tutorials" to his comelier female students.

Even when she'd met the occasional decent guy— a novelist who worked part-time in her favorite bookstore, the new assistant principal at the school where she taught English—love had refused to blossom. The men had been just too shockingly different from her earthy, gutsy Gar. But when she'd dated firefighters or other men who at all resembled him, her heart seemed locked up still tighter.

Last month, after several amusing dates with a resonant-voiced radio newscaster, she'd accepted a twenty-ninth-birthday dinner invitation. While getting dressed for the event she'd felt a definite tingle in her body as she'd chosen her underthings, and she'd made up her mind: If the evening were as delightful as she expected it to be, she would make love with him. Here at last was a man with whom it was possible to imagine a delicious night, a serious future.

The evening had begun with drinks at one of her favorite Village bars, and they'd left holding hands. It had been downhill from there. He'd made the mistake of bringing her to a chi-chi restaurant famous for its new American cuisine—most notably, suckling pig spit-roasted in an open pit before the diners' eyes.

When they were seated right in front of the pit, she'd expressed dismay at having to see the poor trussed beast spinning over the flames, and he'd teasingly called her a hypocrite; she ate bacon and ham, after all. Fair enough, she'd replied, but pigs were Dannie's favorite animal, and if he didn't mind awfully much, she'd rather move to a table with a different view. He'd snapped back that he'd tipped the maître d' twenty dollars for the ringside seats. He'd then suggested that she try to overcome her "unhealthy obsession" with her daughter by sending her to boarding school.

Lying alone in her bed that night, Carrie had decided that sexual attraction was the worst possible criterion for choosing a man. In fact, the whole damned business of trying to fall in love again was doomed at the inception. She should consider herself lucky to have had seven years of romance, and not expect lightning to strike twice.

But Dannie still needed a father. Carrie vowed there and then to make an all-out, do-or-die effort to find him—a decent man, but more settled than her novelist; a man who loved children, but more attractive than the assistant principal; a man who, like her, hated being alone and would be thrilled to find a . . . friend.

And so she'd ended up booking a chalet at The Ladders for a week.

If she were ever going to find her male counterpart, it was likely to be here, among the sheltering pines. The brochure boasted of Six Har-Tru and Two All-Weather Tennis Courts, Our Fabled Vermont Breakfasts Featuring Cob-Smoked Bacon, and the Spring-Fed Pool in the Shadow of Sugarbush Mountain. But its real lure lay in its reputation as the Resort for Single Parents Who Would Rather Be Playing Doubles.

The partnerless-parents-only week ahead offered a cornucopia of activities designed to break the ice: Toga Night, round-robin tennis doubles, a supervised sleep-out for children (clearly designed to allow their parents to sleep around), and an after-dark skinny dip. Tonight's mixer was probably the most important, though. Carrie knew the women would outnumber the men—they always did at singles events—and the halfway-decent men would be snapped up like designer dresses among seconds at a sale.

"Here goes," she said aloud as she detoured around the "spring-fed pool"—which smelled suspiciously of chlorine—where a lone female swimmer cut rhythmically through the turquoise water.

The sounds of singledom filtered out between the sliding glass doors of the adjacent sports and entertainment complex. Ice clinking in tall drinks, forced laughter, a pianist trilling out standards for an indifferent audience—how well she knew the medley!

Pull off this venture, she reminded herself, and you'll never have to hear it again. Plastering a bright smile on her face, she went in.

There were perhaps fifty people milling around the lounge, collecting their "gratis mixed drinks" from the harassed-looking bartender, pretending interest in the inevitable meatballs on the buffet table, engaging each other in verbal Ping-Pong in front of the monotonously flickering electric logs in "our quarrystone fireplace." Scanning the throng, taking in beards, moustaches, bald heads, and half-exposed chests, Carrie looked for the man who would make a decent companion for her and a loving father for Dannie. Just remember, she cheered herself on, you need only one.

Her eyes stopped. Her breathing stopped. Her heart hammered like a bongo drum.

On the far side of the lounge, leaning insolently in a doorway, a tall, reedy man with straight wheat-colored hair and flagrantly upper-class cheekbones stood surveying the room. Arms folded across his chest, he radiated an air of self-containment that set him apart from the restless crowd.

Trying to fathom the extraordinary impact he was having on her nervous system, Carrie decided he had to be the owner of The Ladders. No, she decided a moment later, he was an owner, period—one of those arrogant men who considered the planet their personal domain, who took charge of every situation.

Conceding that he was easily the handsomest man in the room, she murmured a prayer of thanks that she finally knew enough to stay away from his type. He was undeniably well-bred, but so had been a certain stockbroker who'd suggested Carrie spend a week in Eleuthera with him and another woman. He was clearly intelligent, but so had been her neighbor the lecherous professor.

Come to think of it, he was a virtual composite of all the heartless males she'd come here to escape. The insolent posture; the slightly too long, too expensively cut hair; the sculpted mouth that hovered on the verge of a sneer or a smirk: she knew this man. He was like deadly posion in a crystal decanter. He should be forced to wear a label.

Persuading her eyes to focus elsewhere, she found a pleasant-looking medium-sized teddy bear of a fellow covertly glancing her way. Now, this was more like it! she thought, taking in the endearingly untidy brown curls, slightly bashful brown eyes, and unassuming posture. The man almost radiated cuddliness, kindness, stability, and apple pie. He was the sort of man she'd come here in hopes of finding.

He flashed a tentative grin, and she could tell he was working up the nerve to approach her. She gave him an encouraging wave.

Before he could get to her, the tall blond man

had materialized in her space, smiling triumphantly. She thought instantly of two men on the streets of New York vying for a taxi—one politely raising his hand to signal; the other ignoring him as the cab pulled up, then jumping into the back.

Run! she commanded herself, but the man's piercing gray eyes were riveting her in place like a cosmic ray from one of Dannie's TV cartoons.

"Hullo," he said, making much of the word, stressing the first syllable in an unmistakably British accent.

"Hullo, yourself," she returned, coolly mocking, as adrenaline coursed through her body, telling her to ready her defenses. This man staring down at her, exuding Empire as if it were his personal scent, made her feel like a very small country challenged by a very powerful army.

"I've got a fantastic idea," he went on, smiling lazily, dripping breeding and languor.

"Have you?" she drawled. Looking away, she sought the teddy bear's eyes, but his gaze was defeated now; any minute he would try to hail another taxi. She would tell the Englishman she was off-duty and then go after the teddy bear. But what an enticing aroma of citrus and spice surrounded the Englishman! And what intriguing eyebrows he had—broad golden stripes.

"Let me guess what you had in mind," she said, clasping her hands behind her back. "We jump into the pool with our clothes on? Or find the circuit-breaker and kill the lights?"

"Oh, even more outrageous than that." His gray eyes twinkled silver—celestial traffic lights changing to Go. "I was thinking," he said, reaching out an aristocratically thin finger and waggling Carrie's tip-tilted nose, "that we could go directly to Act Three. We find ourselves an amenable justice of the peace and get married. Then, instead of spending the week fighting the inevitable, we could have a glorious New England honeymoon. Of course, if you insist," he rattled on, "we could have the honeymoon first. But I think it would be better for the children if we got married."

Caught up in his inspired silliness in spite of herself, Carrie pretended to consider his proposal.

"I don't know," she began. "I love you with all my heart, but you're much too tall for me. Besides, you're English and I'm Irish."

"And don't leave out that you're a woman and I'm a man." His fingers found their way to her throat, setting a pulse beating jaggedly there. "How are we going to handle that terrible difference?"

Swallowing, she managed to get out around a suddenly thick tongue, "Yes, that's the real problem, isn't it?"

His penetrating eyes went still, giving him an air of almost supernatural intensity. He's trying to read my soul, she thought, recalled to wariness, and she summoned her own powers to throw up a smoke screen.

"Have all your wives had dark hair?" Her voice dripped saccharine.

"I insist on it," he said airily, as though she'd posed the most reasonable question in the world. "Sun and shadow, yin and yang, sweet and sour—there's nothing like a wedding of opposites. Have you ever tried marriage to a fair-haired man?"

"Not even once." She saw a small patch of beard near his right sideburn that had escaped the evening razor, and it provoked an unsettling feeling of intimacy. "Unless," she said, tilting her head, "you mean fair-haired in the metaphorical sense."

He ran a suggestive finger back and forth across his lower lip. "I never did think much of metaphors. As they keep exhorting me on American television, you ought to try the real thing."

Carrie sensed a subtle shift in the air around them. She knew from experience what it was: The other men and women were chalking her and this man up as an item. Time to put an end to that potentially costly misapprehension.

"Frankly, beloved," she said crisply, "I think we should skip the marriage and go straight to the divorce. We don't have a thing in common."

"Don't we?" he challenged softly. His hand closed around the smooth flesh of her slender upper arm, sending electrical currents jumping from cell to cell, making her feel him all the way down to her toes. "Which one of the scintillating men around here is more your type?"

Compressing her lips, unable to believe how her left arm sizzled, she said, "All of them."

"Oh, I see. It's like that." His gray eyes narrowing, he looked puzzled and pensive for a moment, then something seemed to click into place in his mind. "Now that I think of it," he said, "I suppose you're right—we're hopelessly incompatible. That being the case, why don't we team up and try to find each other mates? Strength in numbers and all that, don't you know." He let go of her arm.

Expecting a completely different line, she was momentarily knocked off guard. She threw back her head and laughed. "Are you serious?"

"Why not?" he countered. "Finding partners is much too ghastly a business to handle alone. Besides, as long as I'm hovering around you, you'll keep in mind what it is you've got to watch out for in a man. Good looks, forceful personality, professional success, a devastating second serve—"

"And unbearable conceit," she cried out.

"Exactly. I knew I could count on you to be honest, and my sensitivities be damned. Perhaps you can even remake me and help me be more worthy of love. Tell me, what do you think of this sports coat? Is it going to attract the right sort of woman?"

She reached out and fingered the wheat-colored raw silk. "It's a little too obviously subtle, if you know what I mean. Overly understated. Inversely snobbish. And it's clear that you got it to match your hair. Any woman with her wits about her is going to see it as a danger signal."

Putting his hand lightly on her shoulder, he steered her toward the bar. "I suspected as much. I'll burn it in the morning. May I speak freely about your dress?"

She started to answer, but her vocal cords seemed to be temporarily out of commission. That cool hand on her bare skin was having the peculiar effect of making some parts of her body feel wide open and others cauterized. Finally she managed to clear her throat. "Go ahead."

"I like the fabric," he said analytically, "but I'm not sure those fashionably loose lines do your figure justice." He placed his hands on either side of her waist, bunching the excess yellow material. "You want to wear something that advertises how slender you are here." One impudent hand slid familiarly over her buttocks as he added, "And how beautifully rounded here. As for up here," he went on, fingering the spaghetti straps and gathered bodice, "I like the way it leaves your throat and shoulders bare, but I think those pleats are squashing your breasts. You want to show them off."

Flushing feverishly, feeling as though she'd just been run over by a steamroller—only why was total destruction so luxurious a sensation?—she slapped his hand away.

"Then I suppose that woman over there is your ideal type," she exclaimed witheringly, pointing out a statuesque redhead whose sleeveless black T-shirt and white cropped pants looked as though they'd been sprayed on her voluptuous body.

He raised his arresting eyebrows. "Delectable," he murmured. "You must contrive to introduce us."

"And what about a man for me?" Putting her hands on her hips, she tried to ignore the tightening in her stomach.

"I saw you eyeing that fellow with the curly hair," he suggested.

"Oh—my teddy bear?"

"That sounds right," he said. "Innocent, safe, machine-washable, and no one could call that red velour shirt overly understated. But why don't you and I have a drink first and tell each other the story of our lives?" he went on smoothly, ignoring her suspicious glance. "If our chosen ones think we're attracted to each other, they'll be all the more intrigued. My name is James Luddington and I'm going to drink a black velvet. How about you?"

Mocking his dandy's mixture of Guinness stout and champagne, she opted for the classic coolness of Stolichnaya vodka with soda over crushed ice and lime. Drinks in hand, they threaded their way through the crowd to a small table that gave them a view of both the pool and the crowd.

He raised his frothy mug in a salute. "To finding love," he said grandly.

She felt as though he'd read her secret diary and was throwing it in her face.

"Oh, heavens," she burst out, "let's drink to almost anything else. To peace in the world, to our children, to the Yankees winning the World Series—" Aware that he was staring at her intently, she broke off abruptly. Trying to soften the intensity of her reaction, she touched the rim of his glass with hers and took a sip.

"That bad, eh? Want to tell me about it?"

"No," she said. She swallowed the vodka, cherishing the icy, clean-tasting smoothness in her throat. If he had pressed her just then, she would have remained obdurately silent. But he nodded understandingly, and a door seemed to open inside her. "Yes."

She told him about the two maddening years she'd spent trying to find a man who would make her feel the deep emotions Gar had aroused. By turn grunting sympathetically and laughing at her anecdotes, James Luddington made a good audience, and she told him more than she'd meant to.

"Then I realized they broke the mold after Gar was created," she wound up. "And I decided I would be happy enough if I found a man who would love Dannie as a daddy and me as a friend."

"It was a good marriage, then?" He eyed her over the rim of his mug.

"It was a lovely marriage." She looked away, swallowing hard, but somehow not wanting to stop talking.

"And you and he—"

She shook her head. "Not a divorce. He died." Hurrying on to spare him the obligatory, uncomfortable "I'm sorry," she said, "I was just devastated at the time, but I'm used to it now. It happened three years ago. He was a firefighter. A hero. He died trying to save a child." The phrases rolled off her tongue.

"A hero's widow. That's what they call bittersweet." His gray eyes narrowing, he shook his head. "Pretty rough going for a young mother. Far more bitter than sweet. Tell me"—he toyed with his mug, spinning it, standing it on edge—"are you ever angry at him? Did you consider his death a kind of abandonment?"

Flushing, she said tensely, "I thought you were the man who hated metaphors."

"Touché." But he went on probing. "He was a firefighter when you married him? You knew all the risks?"

"Well, no, actually," she said reluctantly, as if the admission were disloyal to Gar's memory. "We were both planning to be teachers when we got married. He ended up teaching history at a high school in the Bronx—a pretty rough school, but that's where he wanted to be. He cared about those kids. Then it got burned down and one of his students died, and he went into the fire department."

Suddenly she was hearing sirens wailing in her mind. She was smelling the smoke on Gar's skin and hair. "I don't want to talk about him anymore," she said. "Some other time, maybe. Tell me about you."

"I have a six-year-old son named Phillip. That's the most important fact about me. I'm thirty-six . . . go ahead, tell me I don't look it."

"You don't look it."

"I'm British—"

"You look it," she said.

"I lived most of my life in London, but I got lured over here by some people in Boston who think I have a knack with computers."

"Computers! Ugh!" Carrie said. "I'm sorry, that's rude, but I can't help thinking they're the enemy. Dannie loves computer lab at school, but frankly, I wish she were getting Latin instead! You've had this reaction before," she added with a little laugh, noticing the expression on his face.

"Occasionally," he said easily. "I don't mind. But you know how we British are. We get uncomfortable discussing our work in social situations. And this is ever so social, isn't it, my dear Carrie?"

"Ever so," she said dryly. Then, "Do the British have any trouble discussing the cities they live in? Funny, but I can't quite picture you in Boston."

"No? Why not? Can't see me eating baked beans?"

"Oh, it's just my New York chauvinism," she said with a little laugh. "I assumed if you'd been lured to the States, it had to be to Manhattan. You're tall and thin and pale—like our skyscrapers, you see. Boston is too red and stocky."

"Why, Carrie Delaney, I do believe you've just paid me a compliment."

"Never mind," she said crossly. "I'm glad I was wrong. I'd rather have you live in Boston."

Throwing back his blond head, he roared with laughter. "You're a character, you know that? In fact, I live in New Hampshire for the moment. A lot of the Boston computer companies have moved across the border to take advantage of the lower taxes. And a good thing too," he added, lifting his eyebrows, "because it brought me here. Last week when I got notice that my divorce was final, I decided that Phillip and I, along with Mrs. Platt, Phillip's nanny, should celebrate by knocking off for a week of tennis. As I have every intention of marrying again, I decided to cross the river into Vermont and come to The Ladders—for tennis 'and.'"

"Coffee 'and' means coffee with a danish," she teased. "Did you come here for the 'fabled breakfasts'?"

"No, for a danish," he said, straight-faced. "Or a Dutch or Greek or what-have-you—just as long as she'll be mine forever and love my son as her own and maybe have another child with me." A smile tugged at the corners of his mouth. "Of course, my preference is for Irish. There's a history in my family of Irish wives."

"But you were just divorced," she protested, serious.

"Yes, but we sunder our marriages in a less accelerated fashion in Great Britain. First there's a temporary decree, and then, after a waiting period, the final decree. Jenny and I actually separated three years ago. Not to worry. I'm not on the rebound."

She made a face. "I wasn't worried. I'll let the redhead do the worrying." In a softer voice she added, "Were you badly hurt?"

He shrugged, and she noticed that he had wide shoulders for a man of his lean build. "I've never quite made up my mind which is worse—to have a bad marriage end in divorce, or a good one," he said. "Ours was rather nice for a while, until my wife wrote a novel that all the critics went gaga about, and she decided that literature needed her more than Phillip and I did. It was a shock to have her leave, because I'd thought we were both happy. On the other hand, Phillip and I have some decent memories to look back on, and she and I have an easy enough time discussing whatever we have to discuss."

"'On the other hand' gets to be a kind of theme song, doesn't it?" Carrie said wistfully.

She picked up her glass, but it was empty, and she saw that his was too. They had had their drinks and swapped their stories, and now it was time to move on. To her surprise—her dismay—she felt a certain reluctance to get up. It had been a more resonant conversation than she'd had in quite a while. More truths, more laughs.

Watch it, Delaney . . . remember the professor,

the broker, the candlestick maker . . . all those slick, good-looking fast-talkers . . .

"Onward and upward, then," James said gently.

For a crazy moment she thought he had heard her struggling with herself and was taking pity on her; but he couldn't know her that well, couldn't care that much.

"On the way down from my chalet," he went on, "I noticed that several of the tennis courts have lights for night play. I was thinking you could suggest to my redhead and I could suggest to your teddy bear that we play a few games of mixed doubles. Somewhere along the line we switch partners and let nature take its course."

"Play now?" she said doubtfully.

"Why not? We'll all dash home and change—and permit your coach to say, Carrie, that you're not to wear a baggy tennis dress."

"You're on!" she said with a laugh, feeling less alone than she had in a while, delighting in their game.

They stood up, and James caught hold of her hand and kissed it. "You're sure we shouldn't go find that justice of the peace?"

"Of course I'm sure," Carrie cried. "Hasn't every word we've exchanged confirmed how opposite we are? I haven't even said what I think about computers in education, and how they're wrongfully displacing the humanities. I—"

"All right, all right," James interrupted. "I still think we need an independent test. The scientific approach, don't you know. Besides, it will make our two friends wonderfully jealous."

The pianist segued into one of Carrie's favorite songs, "Can This Be Love?" Her head felt light as a cloud.

"What in the world do you mean?" she asked James.

"I'm going to kiss you."

With exquisite slowness he lowered his face toward hers. When his lips found their target, her body arched in a sweet agony of release, as though she'd waited an eternity for this moment of contact.

"Hullo," he murmured in soft surprise against her mouth, setting up delicious vibrations.

"Hullo yourself." She closed her eyes, and her mutinous lips parted, overruling a thousand warning bells. But the hot, probing tongue she awaited in eager dread didn't make itself felt, and her eyes flew open again.

"Carrie," he whispered, trailing small kisses across her cheek. "I want it to be right for you. All of you."

Equal measures of wonder and dismay rose in her. Again came the dangerous illusion: He somehow knew her; he somehow cared.

"Please," she whispered, feeling the center of her being contract.

"Please what? Please more?" His hands were in her hair now, and he smiled at her with surpassing tenderness.

"Please..." Body and mind disintegrating, she

pressed little kisses into the corners of his mouth as though she might find the missing word hidden there. She tasted his lime and spice, and it filled her soul as if it were music. Finally, on the verge of being lost forever, she managed to wrench her mouth from his skin. "Please . . . stop."

Instantly he released her, and his eyes flicked over her face, less tender than mocking now. "Too much feeling for you, my darling?"

She shook her head. "Too much vodka," she mumbled. "That's all. Really."

"I see."

"So I guess your test just proved that I was right," she said, her voice close to steady now. "There can't be anything between us."

"Except friendship," he said. "Our doubles game and all."

"That's right," she said, almost shouting in her eagerness to drown out other messages that were trying to make themselves heard in her mind.

"In the American parlance, we're pals."

"Pals," she echoed. "So I'll go line up the redhead, and you talk to the teddy bear." She held out her hand, and he gave it a vigorous shake. But his other hand went behind his back.

Was she just imagining things, or were his long, aristocratic fingers tightly crossed?

CHAPTER TWO

"MOM, WHAT ARE you doing home?" Dannie asked as Carrie let herself into the chalet. "Weren't you having a good time?"

Carrie swung her pajama-clad daughter around. "Dannie Delaney, sometimes you sound more like a mother than a six-year-old. I came home to change into tennis togs, if you must know. And, yes, I'm having a very nice time."

"Tennis? At night? Honestly?"

"Honestly," Carrie said, smiling at her daughter's wide-eyed curiosity. "Have you forgotten about the great Thomas Alva Edison?"

"Oh, he just invented incandescent bulbs," Dannie announced in one of her breathtaking turnabouts. "I think tennis courts use sodium vapor lights."

Heading into her room, closely trailed by her precocious child, Carrie reached behind her back to unbutton her dress. Catching sight of herself in the mirror, she marveled at the sparkle in her eyes. But, really, the dress was hopelessly baggy.

"Want help with your buttons, Mom?"

"Actually, I'd like privacy, darling." The words were out before she knew it, startling herself as well as Dannie. She had never before felt modest in front of her daughter; they often showered together, and she readily answered Dannie's torrents of questions about the workings of the human body.

Now James's touch had somehow made her different. Oh, but impossible! she told herself, striking down the unwelcome thought.

"I'm in a hurry, you see," she explained, kneeling down and hugging Dannie. "And if you're in here, I'll want to talk with you and kiss you"—she kissed her—"instead of changing my clothes. So you go back out to Gretchen and finish your milk."

"Can I have another cookie? I didn't make it come out even with the milk."

"Yes, you scamp. Just one. And don't forget to brush your teeth." Kissing her again, she said, "Now, please scoot."

She chose a simple white, scooped-neck tennis

dress that was distinguished by a green and white webbed cinch belt. As she hurried through the twilight to the illuminated courts—sodium vapor, indeed!—she hoped that James—no, her teddy bear—would like the figure-revealing dress.

Predictably, redheaded Didi Hayes outrevealed her in a snug-fitting T-shirt and barely-there shorts. James, in that inversely snooty way of his, was wearing ancient bleach-stained wool flannel shorts that had probably been inherited from some titled ancestor who'd played in the first season at Wimbledon. Lew Richards, her teddy bear, compensated for him, though, with shirt, shorts, sweatband, and wristbands that had obviously just been taken from their original packages.

"What a terrific idea!" Lew exclaimed nervously, looking from Didi to Carrie and back again as he took the cover off a world-class graphite racquet. (James's, of course, was well-worn wood.) Glancing up at a lopsided waning moon in a blue-black sky, he said, "I just hope we don't get too much sun."

Didi smiled at him to let him know she found him fantastically clever. "Want me to rub sunscreen all over you, partner?"

"Nah, you might get my racquet greasy." He fiddled with one of the pristine bands at his wrist. "Between shots I'll run to the shade."

"You're sure they're not getting too cozy with each other?" Carrie whispered to James as they went to their side of the court. "I think they're falling in love."

James shook his head. "Not a chance. It's a cover-up for the way they feel about us . . . only they can't yet admit to the feeling. That's why we mustn't move too fast—we'll scare them off. Give them another half-hour of wondering what we're up to, and they'll be absolutely putty in our hands."

She secretly studied the curly-haired man on the far side of the court. "He's cute, isn't he?" she said, flexing her knees.

"He's adorable," James said ferociously, raising his gray eyes heavenward. "How do you like the legs on her?"

"Terrific. I think it's very brave of a woman her age to wear shorts that short."

"Oooh. Low blow, pal. We can't all be twenty-nine." Opening a can of the neon green balls recommended for play at night, James bounced one her way and put two into his pocket. "Pleasant out here, isn't it?"

It really was, Carrie had to admit. They were on one of a pair of Har-Tru courts located between the sports complex and the semi-circle of half-timbered chalets. With lights winking behind drawn curtains, the chalets, which by day had struck her as hokey, looked as snug and inviting as the dwellings in a Swiss mountain village. Beyond the chalets the pines swayed mysteriously, and for a final backdrop there was the dark, soaring majesty of Sugarbush and the rich evening sky gift-wrapped with stars the size of golf balls.

Of course the picture would be even more compelling, Carrie thought, after the four tennis players had changed partners. Statuesque Didi was a perfect match for six-feet-tall James, while she, at five-feet-two, would go very nicely with the medium-sized Lew.

"Tennis, anyone?" James dropped a ball onto the racquet and sent it sailing over the net into the center of the other court.

Lew and Didi both ran for the ball, then each stopped short to let the other get it. It bounced away untouched. James sent a second ball their way. This time they collided . . . and the ball again bounced away untouched.

Carrie couldn't suppress a wicked grin. "They better brush up on their teamwork," she said, "or they won't even last a half-hour."

Lew hit a ball to her, and she sent it back to him with an effortless backhand.

James nodded approvingly. "You know what you're doing out here."

"Oh, I grew up with a racquet in my hand. After Gar died I started playing again as therapy."

"You two didn't play together?" He reached up lazily and caught a forehand of Didi's that surely would have smashed into the fence, and gently lobbed it back to her.

"He hated my mother's country-club scene, and

getting a court in the city is such a hassle. Besides, he said I played to kill. He thought if you were going to play, it should be to have a good time."

James mimed shock. "A good time? What a perversion. Nothing against your husband, of course, but I've never understood people who didn't play to win." Illustrating his philosophy, he ran to the net to get a backhand from Lew and sent the ball hurtling to the baseline.

It was obvious almost immediately that Carrie and James were the superior team. Didi and Lew hit strong shots, but they didn't have the ability to think in the tandem that makes good doubles players. Carrie was frankly amazed that she and James— so different from each other, so incompatible—were able, without a word, to know who should take which shot.

After an uninspired set that they won 6–1, James winked at her and suggested to Lew and Didi that they change partners.

"You be captain," Lew immediately said to Carrie, flashing an engagingly boyish smile. He adjusted his terry-cloth sweatband to capture some straying brown curls. "I may wear my hair like John McEnroe, but the resemblance ends there."

Thrilled to be in the company of someone who didn't think he was the living end, Carrie felt her shoulders relax and her adrenaline level return to normal. "I think we'll do best if I take the forehand court when we're receiving. And you might rush the net more often. I noticed that you always hung around in no-man's-land when Didi served, and that made it pretty easy to get a shot past you."

A look of chagrin crossed his round face and Lew said, "I don't know about rushing the net. I'm always afraid I'll get hit in the mouth. I'm a dentist," he went on, "pediatric, and I hate to tell you what a tennis ball can do to teeth."

"You mean you're the White Mountain Defender?" Carrie cried, invoking the cartoon character she'd seen in various instructive comic strips in Dannie's dentist's office.

"Yeah. And isn't it funny, here I am in Sugarbush basin. Think I'll have to tackle Grotney L. Decay?"

"I'll help you, Defender," Carrie squeaked in the falsetto of his vitamin sidekick, the nervous but valiant "A."

Laughing, they moved into position as James called, "Ready," and prepared to serve.

She was so relaxed that his first serve was bouncing past her before she could get her racquet back.

"Nice," she called out.

"Nice, my eye," Lew muttered. "That was harder than it had to be."

"Wait until you see what I'm going to give him when I'm serving. Bend your knees, Lew."

James won the first game without losing a point. As the two teams were changing sides he whispered to Carrie, "I hope I'm not being too much of a killer. I thought it would help unite you and Lew if you faced adversity together."

His breath was like a sensuous southern breeze against the delicate membranes of her ear. Furious at the trembling in her limbs, at the spiraling heat in her belly, she retorted, "I plan to return the favor. Pal."

Tossing the ball sky-high, her wiry body arching for all it was worth, she sent her first serve spinning furiously to James's forehand. He slammed it back at her, and she returned it cannonlike to the baseline on his side of the court.

His racquet whipped around, and he drove the ball into her alley—and so it went for twelve exchanges, the velocity picking up with each shot, as if they were playing a grudge game of singles and nobody else existed. Finally James changed his tactic and tried to drop a ball just over the net, but instead, it thudded into the net on his side, and Carrie took the point.

Lew applauded softly. "Fantastic. What are you doing out here with us mere mortals?"

"I hope you don't think I hogged the action." Her breathing was ragged and her knees were spongy as she crossed to the other service position.

"Hey, no. The balls all came to you. And a good thing, too, because I don't think I can touch them when they're flying at ninety miles an hour."

But James's shots to Lew arrived at a reasonable speed, as did Carrie's to Didi, and it soon became clear that two separate games were going on at the same time. At the end of the set, which Carrie and Lew won 7–5, the affable dentist suggested that maybe he and Didi should play singles on the other illuminated court while James and Carrie had their own match.

"Now you've done it," Carrie said to James as Lew and Didi moved off.

"What do you mean I did it?" His gray eyes twinkling, he pushed back his straight pale hair.

"Hitting everything to me. Except those pat-a-cake shots to Lew."

James chortled. "In the words of the poet, my darling, it takes two to tango."

"And stop calling me your darling," Carrie said crossly.

The sounds of a leisurely rally came from the other court, and they turned to look at Lew and Didi nicely sending the ball to each other.

"Well-matched," James observed.

"Great. Where does that leave us?"

"Right where we want to be." Dropping a ball onto his racquet and bouncing it into the air, he said, "We broke the ice, we met them, and now we have to keep up the pretense that you and I are an item or else they may feel they've been set up. Remember, it was as a couple that we invited them to play with us."

"Yes, yes," Carrie said, "but the idea was for them to get interested in *us*, not in each *other*. Somehow I thought that at the end of a couple of sets you'd go off with Didi and I'd go off with Lew."

"Believe me," James enunciated in the accented tones of London, "I'm every bit as eager to be alone with Didi as you are to be with Lew. But things have to take their natural course—or at least the appearance thereof. We might stage a fight in front of them, for instance, and stalk off from each other, and then I bet you anything they'd trot after us to offer consolation. Do you think you could convincingly fight with me?"

Carrie folded her arms across her chest. "Without the slightest bit of trouble."

"Terrific." He smiled down at her, his eyes going silvery. "First I think I should kiss you again."

Her heart thudded, and her breathing was as ragged as it had been after that first intense rally with James. Damn! She would have thought the vodka was out of her system by now.

"You mean you kiss me and I struggle with you?" She swallowed hard.

"No, no. You don't want Lew thinking you're cold, do you? And I can't have Didi thinking I'd ever kiss a woman against her will. So first we have a long, intense embrace, really whet their appetites for us, and then we play a couple of games of tennis, and then we have our fight."

"I've got it," Carrie said gleefully. "I could call a serve of yours out—one that was clearly in—and you could challenge me, and we'd take it from there."

"Mmmm . . ." James cocked his head to one side

and then to the other. "Except that anyone who's been around us for even five minutes would know that neither of us would ever argue over a point in a social game, killers though we are."

"Well, maybe we can have a real argument about what to pretend to argue about," Carrie said, her voice tart.

James laughed. "You're absolutely right. I'm being silly. Let's get on with the kiss, shall we? And this time try to act as though you're enjoying it."

"Why, you—"

Still laughing, he brushed the words right off her lips, his mouth so tender that she thought she might swoon. "I can't win with you, my darling, can I?" he whispered against her lips, the vibrations setting off tremors that made every inch of her quake.

His long, supple fingers bit into her shoulders, then contritely erased the pain, and she cursed him more for pretending to care than for having hurt her. Why was it always like this? Why were the gorgeous, clever men self-obsessed and deceitful, quick to do in any woman foolish enough to open her heart?

Meanwhile her mouth had a mind of its own and answered the demanding pressure of his lips with an escalating need. It was as if they were back on the tennis court: The harder the ball came to her, the harder she hit it back. And who, dear heaven, would win the dangerous game they were playing?

On the fringes of her consciousness she was aware that she no longer heard a *thwack thwack thwack* coming from Lew and Didi's court. "They're watching us," she whispered to James as they both came up for air.

"That was the idea, remember? Play it for all you're worth." He put his arms around her and gently kissed her eyelids. "Remember when you were in high school and wanted to be an actress?"

How the devil had he known about that? With her low voice and tendency toward wryness, she'd imagined herself as a second Lauren Bacall . . . only she'd been a small, dark-haired gamine—a cross between Audrey Hepburn and Liza Minnelli, someone had said. But even though she'd gone on to teach literature rather than act it, she still had plenty of ham in her.

Boldly untucking his tennis shirt from his shorts, she insinuated her hand against his bare chest. "I want you. I need you. I must have you," she declaimed with soap-opera throatiness, her hazel eyes growing filmy with desire, her fingers dancing through the soft tangle of his chest hair.

"Oh, Esmerelda," he returned lustily, "how I've longed to hear you say those words." Crushing her against him, he went on fervently. "You're mine then? Only mine? All mine?"

Listening to the strong, steady beat of his heart, she sighed deeply, a kind of peace stealing over her. "As soon as you pass the test, dear Harold," she murmured.

"And what might the test be?" He dropped kisses into her hair.

"It's not for me to tell you. You must consult the oracle on the mountain." That heartbeat was mesmerizing her, turning her mind to mush, her will to modeling clay. Pulling back from his embrace, she said, "I think we're overdoing it. Let's play tennis."

Not moving for a moment, he looked down at her, his eyes probing hers, a small smile on his lips. Then he handed her two balls and said, "Serve them up."

They had long, strong rallies. Not the fierce exchanges of their doubles games, but a steady stroking in which the object seemed to be to match each other's rhythm and keep the ball in play.

They had taken a game apiece when Didi came to the wire mesh fence between the two courts and said, "We've had it. We're both desperate for a drink and a hamburger. Join us?"

Carrie and James looked at each other, recognition dawning. They'd been enjoying their tennis so much, they'd forgotten to stage their fight!

Winking at Carrie, James said to Didi, "Great idea. We'll just play a tie breaker here, and then we'll join you up at the bar."

"What's this all about?" Carrie asked suspiciously as Lew and Didi wandered off. "Look, he's got his arm around her."

James shrugged. "Doesn't prove a thing. You and I were kissing like crazy, and we know how little it meant."

A wave of indignation rising in her, she put her hands on her hips and glared at him.

"Oh, it meant more than a little to you?" he teased softly.

But it hadn't, she told herself. She was just a pretty good method actress, that was all; and a totally invented character named Esmerelda had very much liked the kiss. Had liked it much too much . . .

"I figured I'd be with Lew by now," she protested, "and here I am with you. And if we all have drinks together, I'll never get him alone."

"Shall I level with you?" James put a brotherly hand on her shoulder. "I'm really taking this pal business seriously. I'm not just going to help you find a husband; I'm going to make sure it's the best possible husband. Now, Lew's a nice bloke, but I'm not sure he's made of the right stuff. I think you ought to let me get more of a sense of him before" —he cleared his throat—"before you go on to the next stage."

"I wasn't planning to jump into bed with him the minute you turned your back!" she cried, annoyed. "Just because Esmerelda got a little carried away when Harold kissed her, that doesn't mean I always—" Blushing furiously, knowing how feeble she sounded, she ground to a halt.

She expected James to take advantage of her admission, to let loose a roar of triumph or to simply grab her. Instead, he reached out and ruffled her hair, the way she ruffled Dannie's when the child had embarrassed herself and Carrie wanted her to feel okay.

"So I thought," James went on calmly, "we'd have our drinks, and if he seems to be a good sort, I'll suggest another meeting. Say a picnic tomorrow noon, with our kids. The bigger the crowd, the better the chance you can engage him in a tête-à-tête. Maybe we'll even have races, or a treasure hunt, or play some sort of game that's bound to throw you together."

Carrie regarded him doubtfully. "Are you sure you know what you're doing?"

"I've never been surer."

"It's an awful lot of effort for you," Carrie said. "The picnic, I mean."

"Well, I'm not planning to *make* the tarragon chicken," James said. "We'll go to one of those fancy carry-out places in Waitsfield. As for the games and all, Phillip loves a treasure hunt."

"So does Dannie. They should like each other." But she still felt uncertain.

"And don't forget," James said, "if all goes according to plan, I get Didi." He raised his eyebrows suggestively.

Carrie was relieved and depressed all at once. But anything was better than being alone at the bar, feeling like a specimen being examined on a slide, trading banter with man after man until she found one she trusted—and, of course, you never knew.

"Onward and upward," she said.

CHAPTER THREE

"MOM, HAVE YOU gone crazy?" Dannie asked.

"What do you mean, honey?" Carrie answered brightly as she pushed a wagon down aisle two at the Grand Union in Waitsfield.

"Well, you told me about eleven hundred times on the way up to Vermont that this was going to be a no-cooking vacation. So yesterday we bought Cheerios, apples, oranges, milk, chocolate chip cookies, and frozen pizza," Dannie said, ticking the items off on her fingers. Her wrinkled nose conveyed exactly what she thought of frozen pizza.

"And today," she went on, peering into the wagon, "you're buying flour, sugar, vanilla, eggs. I think there's a mystery going on," she wound up triumphantly.

"You do, do you? Do you suppose the Dannie Delaney detective agency can solve it?" Carrie considered baking powder, baking soda, unsweetened chocolate, and semi-sweet chocolate chips, and ended up taking them all.

"Of course I can solve it!" Dannie jumped up and down, tugging at the wagon, a bright-eyed manic elf in cutoffs and a purple Hunter College Elementary School T-shirt. "I bet you decided you love me sooo much that you just had to make me brownies. Because you're the best mother in the whole world, and you make the best brownies in the whole world. There! Did I solve the case?"

"You just about did, honey. I'm going to bake something—I'm not sure exactly what—for you and for some new friends of ours. We're going on a picnic this afternoon," she added, her voice fluttering a little, "and I said I'd bring dessert. Then I decided that instead of just buying any old thing, I could bake while you're at your tennis clinic this morning."

"What new friends?" Dannie asked eagerly as they headed for the checkout.

"Well, you know how much you like Dr. Wineman? There's a really nice man named Lew Richards who's a kid's dentist. He has curly hair just like White Mountain Defender. And there's a woman named Didi Hayes. She writes for a newspaper in Hartford. She has red hair just like Mara's." Mara was Dannie's best friend back home.

"And, believe it or not," Carrie went on, "there's a six-year-old boy. His name is Phillip. I haven't met him, but his father told me he loves treasure hunts and mysteries. His father's name is James," she ended abruptly, getting into the express lane behind a thin young woman wearing blue jeans and carrying a single quart of low-fat milk.

"Is Lew going to be your next husband?" Dannie asked in her resonant New York City voice, garnering amused stares from other shoppers.

"Dannie Delaney!" Carrie tried to cover her blush by blending over the wagon and plucking out the various items.

"I guess if he's a kids' dentist he must like kids, so I like him," Dannie announced. "I don't like James. I'm going to bring ten Nancy Drew books so I don't have to talk to him." She kicked the wagon.

"Please, darling. Please try not to make up your mind about people before you even meet them. I'm glad you think you'll like Lew, but that doesn't mean you have to decide you don't like somebody else. And could you keep your voice down, do you think?"

The motherly-looking checkout clerk compressed her lips in disapproval. "Eleven fifty-nine," she said as Carrie took out her wallet.

"Well, *you* don't like James," Dannie retorted defensively.

Carrie handed over a twenty-dollar bill. "Why on earth do you think that?"

"You said his name in a weird voice."

"No, I didn't." Confusing feelings welled up in her, and she blatantly changed the subject. "Maybe I *will* make brownies. I was thinking about a chocolate-chip cake with fudge icing, but that's not very practical for a picnic, is it?"

"Make brownies, please? You can put the chocolate chips right in them. I love it when you do that."

Brownies it was, and apples cored and baked whole in a simple orange-juice crust Carrie's mother had taught her to make. Considering that she was working in a strange kitchen, she thought both desserts came out well, the brownies moist and chewy and the apple dumplings golden and fragrant.

While they cooled on the L-shaped wooden counter that divided the kitchen from the living and dining areas, Carrie took a long bath, touched up her toenails with Berry Rich, and paced in front of her closet. Hmmm.

The trouble was, she had no idea about Lew's taste and too many ideas about James's. He would think the short blue culottes looked like a gym suit ... the lime overalls were disgracefully baggy ... and he'd find her red and white checked shirt and form-fitting jeans altogether too enticing.

She decided on the shirt and jeans anyway. Lew couldn't fail to like them.

The group was to have assembled in front of James's chalet, where his silver Renault station wagon was parked, but when the Delaneys arrived, exactly on time, only the tall Englishman and his son were there.

James was wearing a silvery-gray shirt with his ancient Levis, and Carrie snorted inwardly. How like the conceited character to buy clothes and cars to match his eyes. Thank heavens she'd been smart enough from the very beginning not to get involved with someone who was so involved with himself.

Tearing her eyes away from him, she held out her hand to a small blond boy whose bangs, in the British tradition, hung down into his eyes. "You must be Phillip. I'm Carrie, and this is Dannie. She's six too."

The children stared sullenly at each other, and Carrie's heart sank. It was like that between kids—instant affinity or allergy. Or maybe Dannie, already possessed of female intuition, sensed that Phillip was going to grow up to be a dangerous man like his father. Carrie swallowed a giggle at the thought.

Just then Lew and Didi came running down the road in tennis clothes.

"Sorry we're late," Didi called cheerfully. She was panting, and her fair skin was damp. She held up a bag. "All set in the drinks department."

"Were you out on the court?" Carrie asked Lew.

He nodded, grinning boyishly, and she added, "I hope you kept your knees bent." A scarlet flush burst into bloom on his round cheeks, and she gulped. Had he and Didi been playing more intimate games than tennis? Was it too late for her?

She looked at James with desperate eyes, but it was Dannie who came to her rescue.

"I want to sit on Lew's lap in the car," the tyke announced, countering James's suggestion that she and Carrie ride in the front with him and share a seat belt. "And Mama next to us, then Didi. Phillip can have the front seat to himself," she added. "In case he gets carsick."

"Dannie!" Carrie said, chiding the rudeness even as she silently applauded the proposal.

Phillip stuck out his tongue at Dannie. "If I get sick, it'll be from looking at you." He put his hand on his throat and made retching sounds.

James winked at Carrie. "Now you kids are even," he said mildly, "and we can get on with having fun. We'll sit the way Dannie suggested; and, Phillip, you can make the next arrangement that comes up. Let's hit the road, everyone. Time to get into the bus."

Sitting with her blue-jeaned thigh touching Lew's bare leg, Carrie felt suddenly tongue-tied. But as James deftly guided the car down the Sugarbush access road and headed south on Route 100, Dannie made up for her mother's silence with incessant chatter.

"Are you really a kids' dentist?" she asked in the awed tones an adult would have reserved for an astronaut. Leaning against Lew's shirt, she cooed, "Smell my breath. I floss after every meal, and I always use fluoride toothpaste. I like carrots and apples much better than cookies and candy."

To Carrie's delight, Lew put his arms around Dannie and indulgently praised what he had to know were exaggerations. Happy to let them begin to make a relationship, she tried to engage Didi in conversation. After all, she reminded herself, being pals with James was a two-way street. She had to make sure the redhaired reporter for *The Hartford Courant* wasn't a potentially heartbreaking best-selling novelist like James's ex-wife.

With a pleasant laugh Didi assured her that she had no interest in writing fiction. Frankly confessing to being thirty-five, she said she wanted to be on the city desk of *The New York Times* when her fortieth birthday came. By then her twin daughters would be starting college, and joint custody would no longer mean she and her ex-husband both had to live in Hartford.

The animated redhead grew glum as she mentioned her ex-husband, and Carrie instantly understood. Didi was still carrying a torch. So she'd glommed onto Lew in hopes of extinguishing it, and he, being human, had gallantly obliged. She'd probably have to sample several different men before she was ready to commit herself again. Which

meant that both she and Lew were still available
... but she might hurt James, who was eager to
settle down ... oh, heavens, how complicated mating was.

James took them west into the Green Mountain
National Forest, describing a waterfall and secluded
picnic area he and Phillip had once explored.

The spot lived up to the expectations he'd raised.
A narrow stream of water tumbled down between
spruce trees, making a joyful roar, the spewing white
foam a brilliant contrast with the blue-gray rocks
over which the stream skittered. At the base of the
falls a calm, shallow pool sparkled in the dappled
light, hinting at trout and inviting bare feet.

Under the generous branches of an old oak tree,
a single picnic bench of weathered wood sat waiting
for them. And for the moment at least they had the
place to themselves without the intrusion of civili-
zation.

Forgetting how dangerous it was to compliment
a conceited man, Carrie exclaimed to James, "It's
glorious here! Perfect!"

"Isn't it just?" he said smugly, as though he'd
personally carved the stones and set the water flow-
ing. "We could come back one night and camp out—
all of us, of course," he added hastily, catching
Carrie's wary look. "There's a fireplace on the far
side of the table and a clear space for sleeping bags."

James placed his arm around Carrie's shoulders
and went on, "The third week in August is the best

time of the year to see shooting stars, you know. We could wish up a storm."

She watched dreamily as Didi and Lew wiped off the picnic table and started to set out lunch. Dannie was sitting on a moss-covered log, reading a Nancy Drew mystery. Phillip threw stone after stone into the stream.

"What would you wish for?" she dared to ask. "A thousand and one nights with Didi?"

His eyes went opaque. "Is that what you want me to wish for?"

"Well, she is pretty nice. Nicer than I thought she was." James's arm tightened around her, and she leaned her head against him, the pounding of blood in her ears as loud as the roar of the tumbling stream.

It was so different from leaning against Gar, who at five feet seven couldn't help but offer the un-hospitable bony part of his shoulder. James held her against his chest, offering hardness and softness at once, supporting her yet yielding. A good quality in a . . . pal.

Phillip came running up to them, his butter-colored hair bobbing. Carrie's fingers itched to push back his bangs. "Father," he began in his sweet British piping, "will you show me how to skim stones? Mine keep on going *plop*."

"Sure, I will," James said, radiating fondness. "It's all in the wrist. Shall we give Dannie a lesson too?"

Phillip shook his head vehemently.

"Never mind," Carrie said quickly. "I thought she and I might go gather a centerpiece of some sort for the picnic table."

James gave her a look she couldn't quite fathom. "A killer on the courts, a peacemaker in the woods. You're an intriguing woman, Carrie Delaney." Before she could answer he took his son by the hand and led him down toward the water. "Now, you want to pick the flattest stone you can find," she heard him say. "Then you hold it between your thumb and forefinger like this—"

In her sternest interior voice she reminded herself that history was full of men who were good with children and impossible with women.

Her own father, Jack Benden, had been cut from the same pattern. He'd thought nothing of flirting with other men's wives at the playground while he fondly watched Carrie and her two sisters cavorting on the jungle gym. Openly involved with a young, single neighbor, he'd gone on living with Carrie's mother, Maureen, "for the sake of the children," even though the setup had brought equal misery to his wife and his mistress.

He'd died before Carrie had met Gar, but she didn't need to see the two men side by side to realize she was, quite deliberately, marrying her father's opposite. And James and her father, with their gift of gab and greedy kisses, would have probably gotten on famously, enchanging pictures of their children while they drank black velvets and eyed the legs of passing women.

By the time lunch was over, Carrie was feeling less than sentimental about children herself.

Just as she had been about to seat herself between Dannie and Lew, hinting at a happy family unit, Phillip had said since Dannie got to assign the seats in the car, he would arrange the table . . . men on one side, women on the other. Carrie received several gratifying leg nudges, but she had a suspicion they came from James, not from Lew.

Dannie had said the tarragon chicken that James had bought was barfo disgust, and Phillip had dumped his apple juice over the arrangement of pine cones, ferns, and stones Carrie and Dannie had made for the centerpiece. When Carrie had unveiled her home-baked desserts, Dannie had made goo-goo eyes at Lew and virtuously said, "I wish grown-ups wouldn't tempt kids with sweets." Lew had been about to reach for a brownie, but instead he'd had to share an unadorned pear with Dannie, while James, Phillip, and Didi devoured the goodies.

Looking as though he'd never had a better time, James proposed his treasure hunt. They would divide into three teams, split up for an hour, and see which side could bring back the most items from a list he'd prepared.

As he scribbled names on scraps from a note pad and dropped them into a paper bag, he gave Carrie one of his sly winks, and a tremor of excitement ran through her. He would contrive to make her and Lew a team, and he would be with Didi . . . oh, but that would leave the children on their own, which of course wouldn't do.

Phillip jumped up and down. "Let me pick, Father, please."

"All right. Whomever you pick is your teammate, unless you pick yourself or Dannie. If you do, you'll have to try again."

Phillip drew Didi's name and looked shyly pleased. Carrie found to her astonishment that she was very relieved. Imagining James and Didi off in the woods, even for an hour, didn't sit well with her.

Dannie's turn came next, and she picked . . . Lew. She ran over to him and hugged his leg.

That left James and Carrie to go off to the woods together. Relief seeping away, she turned accusing eyes on him. He raised his broad eyebrows to suggest surprise, then frowned down at the traitorous paper bag.

But what was done was done, his expression suggested, and he handed out copies of the treasure list. One leaf that had turned an autumn color (20 points) . . . one pine cone free of pitch (15 points) . . . a stone with an unbroken band of white encircling it (10 points) . . . a big fat juicy worm (5 points).

He warned against poison ivy, and the teams were off.

Carrie tried to force her eyes to search for leaves

and worms, her mind to dwell on the beauty of nature. But she kept being drawn back to the beauty of James's body as he led her up a winding, blue-blazed trail that climbed alongside the rushing falls. He even looked like an owner out here in the woods, damn him, as he gracefully ducked under low branches and loped across the trickling rivulets that branched off from the stream.

With a delicious fearfulness, she half expected him to stop and take her in his arms. But he went on playing jolly camp counselor, exhorting Carrie to keep up the pace and drawing her attention to this brilliant patch of moss, that lightning-charred tree. She could hear happy shouts from Dannie and Phillip somewhere nearby, but the noise was totally obscured by the dense spruce and pine. She told herself she was having a delightfully innocent time.

When they were all the way above the falls, parallel to a level stretch of the stream, James stopped and reached back for Carrie, but only to point out a phenomenon of nature. On the far side of the water, a maple tree stood waving, all its leaves a fulsome green except for a single scarlet branch that stuck out over a rock pool, soaking up the sun.

Carrie laughed delightedly. "It looks like a woman who's dyed one streak in her hair."

"Doesn't it just? Listen, you tarted-up maple, I'm going to pluck one of your leaves."

"What do you mean?" Carrie cried in alarm as he made a move toward the stream.

"That's why I brought you up here," he said. "I glimpsed that scarlet branch while we were having lunch. There's no trail on the other side of the water, you see, but the stream is flat right here, and I can just pop across."

"Are you out of your mind?" She reached forward and crooked a finger through one of his belt loops, halting him.

He grinned at her, his eyes as bright as the dazzling water. "Probably. But don't you want to win the treasure hunt? I can tell you, the prize is fabulous—a squirt gun in the shape of the state of Vermont. I'm going to win it for you, little lady. Don't worry about me on those rocks. I'm wearing my trusty crepe-soled hiking boots." He lifted a blue-jeaned leg to prove his point.

Calmly disengaging her finger from his pants, he dropped a single small kiss onto the tip of her nose. He rolled up his jeans two notches and started across the stream.

Her stomach lurching, Carrie held her breath as she watched his progress. He was as sure-footed as a goat, but—oh, heavens—the water was surging around him, and those rocks must be as slippery as ice. If he fell . . . She momentarily closed her eyes against a dread vision of his beautiful body being swept down over the falls and pounded by the heartless stones.

He made it to the other side, plucked a single red leaf, and gave Carrie a triumphant wave. Starting jauntily back toward her, he grinned a hero's grin for imaginary television cameras.

And put one foot on a rock that came loose, and fell into the roiling water.

"James!" Carrie shrieked, clambering down the bank.

"The water's fine! Come on in!" he called, unfolding himself and standing up, his saturated clothes clinging to his body.

"Idiot!" she yelled, her panic turning to fury.

"It's all right. I'm wearing swim trunks underneath!" His grin intact, he started toward her, then a log floating downstream clipped him behind the knee, and he fell back into the water.

When he stood up again, Carrie could see he was racked with shivers, and the grin was somewhat askew. His movements toward her slowed down, and he seemed to be foundering. With a start she realized the stream bed had suddenly gotten deeper, the current stronger, the slippery stones more treacherous.

Yanking with all her might at an overhanging spruce branch, she managed to get the elastic limb down within his grasp. His movements still languid—this preposterous man!—he pulled himself to safety just as the current surged around him and threatened to sweep him over the falls.

"Oh, Lord, James, I thought you were going to be killed!" she sobbed, tearing open his drenched and icy shirt, frantically trying to heat his chest with kisses.

"It was worth it for the cure," he said with a great

sigh, pressing her head against him, humming contentedly as her lips zigged and zagged across his skin and she brokenly repeated his name. "And look, my darling. I managed to hold on to the leaf. Am I not a right and proper hero?"

She pulled back abruptly and looked. Smiling like a small boy, seeming not to know he was vibrating with shivers, he held up one very wet but undeniably scarlet maple leaf.

Something broke in her as a memory surged up from the past and walloped her in the chest: Gar grinning for the tabloid photographers seconds after he'd emerged from an inferno of a tenement, into which he'd gone to save a small boy's hamster. As the cameras had clicked, the building had collapsed. Another thirty seconds inside, and Gar would have died.

And the next time he had died...

"Dammit!" she screamed, hammering at James with clenched fists. "I don't want to be in love with another hero!"

Suddenly silence fell between them, the pounding of the water over rocks the only sound in the world. James cupped her chin and forced her to meet the steely silver of his eyes.

"Say that again," he commanded.

"No," she whimpered. Her hands dropped to her sides.

He let go of her, and for a terrible moment she thought he was going to strike her, so fierce was the expression on his face. But instead, he enfolded her with a tenderness that wounded her more deeply than any blow could have.

"I didn't mean—" she began, but a look from him stopped her cold.

"It's all right," he murmured, brushing her lips with his. "Don't you know how all right it is? I love you, Carrie Delaney."

"No, don't," she pleaded, crying softly.

Leaning her head against his chest, she felt a spasm tear through him that had nothing to do with emotion.

"Oh, heavens, you're freezing," she said in alarm. "We have to get you back to the car."

"We have to get me out of these jeans," he agreed from between chattering lips. Sinking down onto the trail, he began to take off his boots. "Don't worry. I wasn't kidding about having on swim trunks underneath. You never know when you're going to want to go for a dip on a picnic." Wringing out a drenched sock, he added, "Cozy little domestic scene, isn't this? Almost like being married. One minute we're talking love; the next, we're doing laundry."

"Please," she said hoarsely, turning away as he pulled off his jeans. "Please don't."

"That seems to be one of your theme songs. Please don't make my body feel so good. Please don't open up my heart."

She sank down beside him and put her face in her hands.

He slid an arm around her and held her close.

"I'm really not such a bad sort. I can get a letter of recommendation from my ex-wife."

"Oh, James, you've got to believe me," she begged between sobs. "It can't possibly work." A hiccup turned into a giggle turned into fresh sobs.

"I'm afraid my handkerchief is wet," he said, "so I'll have to kiss away your tears." Doing so, he brought his lips down to hers, and she tasted the salt on his tongue. Her frantic fingers caressed him, kneaded him, dug into him as their mouths fused and their tongues danced wildly around each other.

"Why can't it work, my darling?" he murmured into her ear. "Doesn't your every instinct tell you we were made for each other?"

Opening her eyes, she shook her head frantically, even as the sight of his near-naked long-limbed body sent a sugary heat surging through her veins. "You're too much like Gar. In the wrong ways. I just can't become involved with another man who's going to go and get himself killed."

"If I promise never again to walk across a waterfall?" He kissed the corners of her eyes.

"Then it will be something else. Rescuing a kitten from a tree, or rewiring a computer bare-handed . . . And if you're not risking your body, it'll be more recklessness of the spirit."

"What recklessness of the spirit?" He folded indignant arms across his bare chest.

Eyes dry, she regarded him balefully. "Telling someone you love her when you've known her less than twenty-four hours."

"My dear woman, I've known I loved you since our very first kiss. Maybe since the moment I first set eyes on you in your shapeless yellow dress. So I think I've been the epitome of responsibility, not saying a word until now. Besides," he went on, his grin growing wider, "you said the words first. You verily pounded them into my chest. Shall I refresh your recollection, as they say in court? The exact words were, 'I don't want to be in love with another hero.' The defense rests."

Color ebbed from her cheeks. "You're not going to hold me to that," she protested. "It was just that I was so panicky for a moment. You really came close to going over the falls."

"Or maybe some of that vodka you drank last night is still in your system," he suggested with undisguised sarcasm.

She stared off into the distance, watching the hypnotic swaying of the pines, tracing a stray ray of sunlight across a rock, following the flight of a small warbling bird up into the sky. Turning at last to face James, she soberly met his eyes straight on.

"I know what you think—that I'm a coward," she said. "Running from the risks of love. But it isn't just that. There are . . . other things. My father. I mean, I know there are no guarantees in life, but I want the odds in my favor. That whoever the next man is for me, he won't wake up one morning and follow some other pair of legs down the road."

"Does a man have to have lived as a monk to earn your trust?" James asked, his eyes blazing. "You'd like to peg me as some kind of world-class womanizer because you don't want to admit that every kiss we've shared has knocked off your socks. Put it down to my unholy practiced skills, not to your own response."

"Stop telling me what I'm really all about," she burst out. "The fact is, whether you want to acknowledge it or not, the man I'm interested in is Lew. Look how Dannie's taken to him," she said eagerly, clinging to the fact as if to a lifeline. "You have to admit it, James, you haven't made a big hit with my daughter, and I don't think Phillip likes me any better. And they really can't stand each other."

He shrugged. "I'm not worried about the kids. We could turn them around in a second. But I'll be damned if I'll see you at war with yourself over me. Maybe if you really get it on with Lew you'll come to your senses." He sighed. "But what a waste of time, my darling. Life is so short. I don't want to give up thirty seconds that I could spend with you."

He put his arms around her and pulled her on top of him. "Promise me you won't rule me out. Tell me this feels as good to you as it does to me." Unbuttoning her red and white checked shirt, he freed her silk-clad breasts, then held her tight so they pressed against his chest.

Closing her eyes, letting her lips drift down to his, she longed to yield to the gorgeous warmth that filled her body and spirit. But she thought of the look on her mother's face when her father hadn't come home for dinner . . . sometimes hadn't come home until breakfast. She thought of the unreachable side of Gar, the glint his eyes had only when he was living the part of his life that had nothing to do with her or Dannie.

Reluctantly pulling back from James, she pleaded, "If you care about me, you'll help me get Lew. He's exactly the man I came to Vermont to find. But really help me this time. Did you rig the names in the bag somehow so you and I would end up out here together?"

"You little devil, what a devious mind you have. Okay. I confess. I did. I didn't write either of our names on a slip, and I wrote Lew's and Didi's three times each and counted on the law of averages to do the rest."

She nipped at his neck. "You're a terrible man. And, oh, heavens, you're starting to shake again. We have to get you out of here. Lew brought a sweater with him. I'm sure he'll lend it to you."

"You're already talking like his wife," James said sourly. "I think that's what's making me shake."

"Is this your idea of being helpful?" Her hazel eyes narrowed.

"All right," he said with a sigh, trying to sound gracious. He got to his feet, brushing off leaves and dirt. "Whatever makes you happy."

Carrying his jeans, shirt, shoes, and one scarlet maple leaf, they started down the trail toward the others.

CHAPTER FOUR

AT FIVE O'CLOCK the telephone rang in the chalet, and Carrie leaped for it.

"Hello?" she said eagerly.

"Hello, my darling pal," said a cheeky British voice—a voice she suddenly felt she'd known all her life. "I hope you're not going to break my heart and tell me that breathless greeting was in expectation of a call from the dry cleaner."

Stretched out on her bed like a teenager, hugging a pillow beneath her chest and her legs bent at the knee, she admitted that it was his call she'd been waiting for.

"Just because I was worried about you," she amplified quickly. "As any friend would be. You were pretty pale when I last saw you."

"Mrs. Platt made me a restorative cup of tea."

Mrs. Platt had been Phillip's nanny when he was an infant, and after James's wife had left, she'd come back to "do" for the Luddington males. Carrie hadn't met her, but she pictured permed gray hair, wire-rimmed glasses, a lantern jaw, and a warm heart underneath the stern façade.

"Half tea, half rum, a tablespoon of sugar, and a good squirt of lemon," James went on. "And she made me spend an hour in a hot bath. I wish you'd been here—just for the tea part, of course."

Carrie hugged her pillow harder, her body thrilling at the thought of his lean length languidly stretched out in the warm bath. She forced her eyes to stray to the bedside table, where she'd set a brimming water glass holding one bedraggled scarlet maple leaf. She had no real hope of keeping the leaf alive. It was there primarily to remind her sternly, at moments like this, that James Luddington was Mr. Wrong.

"Will you be up to going to Toga Night?" she asked.

"I said I would, didn't I? Though, good Lord, Carrie, are we supposed to take the instructions literally? Wear bedsheets with nothing on underneath?"

"That's what the invitation says." Carrie looked

at the card with its Greek-style lettering. "'Absence of underwear subject to verification.'"

"It's really the most vulgar thing I've ever heard of," James railed at the other end of the wire.

"If you're nervous, you can wear your all-purpose emergency swim trunks." Carrie oozed sweetness. "Though, of course, you may have to pay some dreadful penalty if you're caught."

"Well, if you're the one who administers the punishment—" James began.

"Never mind that," Carrie said hastily, trying to blot out the delicious fantasy she'd begun to entertain along the same lines. She sat up, thinking a more grown-up and decorous posture might help her keep things straight. "What are you going to do to pry Didi away from Lew?" she asked. "They were holding hands behind my back in the car coming home."

"As well they might have been. They're nicely suited to each other."

"Now, listen, James," Carrie said, her low voice intense, "I like Didi, and I'm sure she means well, but she's only going to hurt Lew. She's still in love with her ex-husband. It's going to take a couple of years and more than a couple of men before she's ready to fall in love again." The more Carrie thought about this theory, the more it made sense to her. "Believe me, I know."

"She's going to hurt Lew, and you're not?" James let out a snort, and she knew exactly what he looked like at that moment, his mouth in a mocking grin, his gray eyes crinkling in gentle derision. "You know he's not man enough for you, Carrie. Even if he thinks he is and decides to take you on, two weeks or two months or two years from now you'll realize what it's all about, and that will be the end of poor Lew."

Carrie opened the drawer of the night table and rummaged for cigarettes, only to remember that she'd quit smoking nine years ago that month. Everything happened to her in the summer. First love . . . last cigarette . . . her wedding . . . the birth of Danielle McGrath Delaney, seven pounds, eleven ounces. And now summer was almost over, there was a definite tang in the air, and she hung suspended between two fates.

"I'll make him happy," she said defiantly. "I do like him."

"I know you do." James paused, and she could almost hear his brain working. "And I know whom you love."

"Dammit," she exploded, "is this how you keep your deals? You're just proving that my suspicions about you are right. I love Dannie, that's whom I love, and I know what I want for us, and I know what I don't want. Are you going to help me or not?"

Holding her breath, she sat waiting for the mocking laugh, the telling retort. Please, she found herself praying inwardly, let him say, "If you want to be a fool, my darling, you're on your own." Let me be over and done with him!

Instead, he apologized profusely—damn him—and promised to do everything in his power to help out. "I'll ask Didi to dance, and I'll charm the pants off her. At least I would if she were wearing pants. And I'll contrive to get her to come away with me."

"How will you do that?" Carrie asked.

"Oh, I'll find a way," James said with his characteristic breezy confidence. "I'll suss out her innermost desire and offer to fulfill it. A double-dip chocolate cone, or something. Since, as you say, I'll be one of many men on her road to happiness, it won't matter if my heart isn't in it."

Carrie had grown so used to his voice, she was scarcely conscious now of his being British. But "suss out" made her smile. She told him so, and he said he was glad because she had a splendid smile. Did she know she had a single dimple next to her right eye that showed only when she was amused?

She told him she had to go see about supper for Dannie, and she did—but on the way she stopped to look in the mirror. She grinned this way and that . . . and saw no dimple. No one had ever mentioned it to her before, not even Gar, who knew every inch of her. Because the dimple didn't exist . . . or didn't exist unless James was there?

He was undeniably the most amusing man she'd ever met. Probably the handsomest, sexiest, and most clever too. If she were looking for a man with whom to have a fling, she doubted she could do better.

But a lifetime was something else.

Keeping that thought front and center in her mind, she went to cook macaroni.

A skinny dark-haired man draped in an Yves Saint Laurent geometric-print sheet swooped down on Carrie. "Do you love my designer toga? Tell me you love it." His breath was generously perfumed with designer Scotch.

"I love it," Carrie said pertly, her eyes sweeping the room for James, Lew, and Didi. "But I thought the management provided only basic white."

"Oh, the management." He rolled his bloodshot brown eyes. "When you've come to as many of these singles' weeks as I have, you'll learn to bring your own sheet. But you look very sweet in white, and I like the pearls," he went on, his voice getting cozier by the minute. Reaching out and fingering her absurd costume just above the green and pink silk scarves she'd twisted into a belt, he leaned over and asked, "Is that the sheet you slept on last night?"

"Beware of Greeks bearing glibness," she muttered, and moved on.

Glancing at the plastic grapevines festooned from the ceiling, she had the uncomfortable impression that she was back at a high school theme dance. But apparently most of the guests at The Ladders thought Toga Night was great fun, for bedsheets abounded—sashed with neckties and clotheslines; accessorized with sandals, running shoes, and one pair of saddle shoes. Sounds of merriment rang through the room.

The staff had opened the folding doors that normally served as a wall between the quarrystone fireside lounge and "our spacious verandaed dining room." Recorded music filled the air, most of it with a Greek theme. Carrie recognized melodies from *Zorba the Greek* and *Never on Sunday*. A few couples were dancing.

A pudgy gray haired man brandishing what looked like a shepherd's crook was making the rounds, flaunting an oversize badge that proclaimed him an official inspector. Watching several women flee from him shrieking, Carrie realized he'd put himself in charge of checking up on compliance with the no-underwear rule.

At last she saw Lew walk into the lounge and pause near the doorway, smiling his boyish smile, tugging at his toga, clearly needing to work up some nerve to enter into the madness. Seized by a zany idea, she ran over to the gray haired "inspector" and charmed him into lending her his props.

Sauntering boldy up to Lew, she flashed the badge. "Hello there, Defender."

"Hi, Carrie." He seemed very glad to find a familiar face. "Can I get you a drink?"

"Why, Defender, is that an attempt to bribe me?" He looked bewildered, and she waved the shepherd's crook. "I'm on duty. Dress-code inspector."

Recognition finally dawned on his round face, and a mottled flush spread over his cheeks. "Er—" he began.

"Never mind," she said hastily, realizing her joke had had the opposite effect from getting him into a party mood. "If you promise not to show me yours, I promise not to show you mine. I'll take you up on that drink though. Vodka and soda with—no, scratch that," she babbled, suddenly on edge. "I'm going to go Greek all the way. I'll have an ouzo on the rocks. Let me just return these silly props, and I'll meet you at the bar."

He had ordered a bloody Mary for himself, and, to her great annoyance, she remembered her father saying that he had no use for a man who drank tomato juice after twelve noon. Since when had her father known what was what in this world? But he had a way of invading her mind like this, at the most unexpected times.

In an effort at tuning him out, she raised her licorice-scented glass and said the first words that came to mind. "I suppose the appropriate toast is . . . to agape and eros."

Lew clinked her glass, then compressed his lips in chagrin. "There I go again," he said, "signing on the dotted line without having read the small print. What's ag-a-pay?"

"It's spiritual love. Sacred love. It comes from the name of a feast the early Greek Christians held in connection with the Lord's Supper."

"Interesting." He sipped at his drink. "And I guess eros is profane love. That sort of covers things, doesn't it?" Shaking his curly head, he emended, "No, it doesn't. It leaves out falling-in-love love. Romantic love. This may sound like a line I dreamed up between fluoride treatments, but, believe it or not, I think there's a difference between romance and sex."

Carrie caught her breath. She'd intended to steer Lew gradually back to that moment, the evening before, when their eyes had first met and he'd evinced definite interest in her . . . to that moment before James, drat him, had monopolized Carrie for himself and thrown Lew and Didi together. But Lew had just given her a conversational opening she couldn't resist.

"There's a gigantic difference between romance and sex," she agreed. Pausing for effect, she went on. "The difference is that romance breaks your heart."

"Wow." He looked shocked. "I didn't think you were the cynical type."

"I'm not. I'm just realistic." She touched his arm lightly. "Do you want to sit down? I'd enjoy talking with you."

"Sure." His big brown teddy-bear eyes swiveling anxiously, he said, "I was supposed to meet Didi here at eight, so let's get a table for four. You're meeting James, aren't you?" His voice left no room for uncertainty. He hoped she was.

"Well, actually, James and I have decided to let things cool down. We have . . . different values."

"You do?" He was sounding more alarmed by the minute. Glancing at his bare left wrist, he laughed nervously. "I forgot, I decided that a watch would look pretty dumb with a toga. I wonder what time it is."

Consulting the clock over the bar, she said, "Eight-twenty. Don't worry, Didi will get here. This is probably her first experience with toga draping."

Carrie led him to a table adorned with a red and white checked tablecloth—perhaps a leftover from Come As Your Favorite Pasta Shape Night.

But where was James? If Didi got there before he did, Carrie was going to have trouble on her hands. She'd gotten off on the wrong foot with Lew this evening, and she had a feeling every time she opened her mouth she was going to put her foot right back in it. She needed her coach—if indeed he came through for her and proved as clever at separating Lew and Didi as he'd been at getting them together.

Meanwhile, the safest thing was to get Lew to do the talking. She wanted to know more about him anyway. Everything she'd learned since she'd first set eyes on him had confirmed her initial impression that here was a gentle, decent man. But it would be nice to have some details.

"Do you spend a lot of time in New York City?"

she asked. She already knew his dental practice was located in Bronxville, in Westchester County, a half-hour from midtown.

"I come in every month to see my son." Wistfully, he added, "If I come in between my visits, I always end up doing something crazy like parking in front of his building hoping I'll see him come out. Someone once asked me if I was a detective on a stake out," he added with a shaky laugh, "because I was just sitting there in my car all afternoon."

"Oh, Lew, how sad. Didn't you . . . couldn't you—" She paused, not wanting to say something hurtful. "It's too bad you couldn't get a custody arrangement that makes you happier."

He pushed his fingers through his endearingly untidy curls. "Remember what I said about signing things without reading the fine print? I guess that's what I did with the custody agreement when Phyllis and I split up. Not that I didn't read it, but I didn't really know what I was getting into. She said the adjustment would be easier for Jason if he got used to thinking of Matt"—his pleasant face contorted, making it plain how much he disliked the man who bore that name—"if Jason could think of Matt as his father," he went on. "Especially since she was already . . . already expecting Matt's baby."

Carrie took his hand and squeezed it. "You deserved better than that."

He shook his head. "I'm not so sure. Jason wasn't

much more than a baby himself, and—it's hard to explain—I've always enjoyed kids when they're, you know, talking and all that—real little people, like Dannie. But babies..." He shrugged. "Babies always seemed so alien to me. Even my own. So when we wrote the custody agreement, I had no idea how much I would miss him. Now, every time a three-and-a-half-year-old boy comes into my office, I kick myself up and down."

A part of Carrie wanted to hug him and stroke him and make the hurt go away. And a part of her thought about James and how he would never, under any circumstances, have surrendered a child of his. But her father had clung to his children, though it would have been kinder all around if he'd made a clean break and married the woman he loved. And Gar had condemned his own child to be fatherless when he'd died trying to save someone else's daughter.

On the other hand ... on the other, other hand ...

"So incredibly complicated," she said aloud.

To her surprise, his eyes brightened. Had she finally managed to say the right thing?

"Do you know," he began, "how good it is to hear someone utter those words? It seems that for the past two years every time I told a woman my story, she'd say, 'I understand perfectly. I know exactly how you felt. A friend of mine went through the same thing.' Thank you for not pegging me."

Coloring guiltily—she had, after all, pegged him

within seconds of first meeting his eyes—she said, honestly enough, "I like you, Lew."

"I like you too, Carrie." He smiled warmly.

Her heart didn't skip any beats, but her mind danced a little jig. In the background the music shifted from Greek-style instrumentals to Frank Sinatra singing "Fine and Dandy." A sign? she wondered hopefully.

"And Dannie adores you," she said.

"She's some kid." Lew grinned.

"I hope we get to see you after this week is over."

"Hey, that would be nice." Leaning forward earnestly, he added, "You've probably already been told this, but Dannie has a class-two overbite. It's cute now, but it's a condition you're going to have to keep under observation, and you'll probably want to consider interventive orthodontics. I know you've got a good dentist in the city—Wineman, Dannie told me; he's one of the best—but if you ever want a second opinion, on the house, just come on up to Bronxville."

Carrie's eyes darted to the various entrances, praying for James to materialize. Orthodontics! Wasn't there anything she could say to the man to get him back on the track of I-and-thou?

"I was thinking more of getting together socially," she tried. "Maybe you'd come down to Greenwich Village for dinner with Dannie and me some night after one of your visits to Jason. I'm a pretty good cook, and this time I'll make sure you get to have dessert. Or bring Jason down to play with Dannie. She's great with younger kids, and we have a rooftop garden complete with a sprinkler. I bet he'd love that."

Moved by her own words, she smiled softly at the picture of urban-but-green family togetherness.

"You're a gardener? Me too," Lew said enthusiastically. "I almost didn't come up here this week because my tomatoes finally ripened. You know," he rattled on, cupping his chin in his hand, "sometimes I think I must live in some kind of microclimate. I've got a friend up in Tuckahoe, he's actually north of me, and his stuff always ripens a good ten days ahead of mine. And I planted Burpee's Early Girls too," he wound up with great animation. When he began to discuss the aphids that were infesting some of his plants, Carrie excused herself and went off to the powder room.

"Delaney, Delaney," she said with a sigh, scrutinizing her reflection in the mirror. Had she forgotten to blend her foundation? Was there spinach caught between her teeth?

No. She thought she looked rather appealing, in fact, as imitation Greeks went. The total effect of ruffled dark hair, luminous hazel eyes, toga, and flat strappy sandals was of a nymph who'd just been chased by Pan through a mythological wood.

But Lew wasn't chasing her. Hardly! In his own sweet way he was running as fast as he could—the other way.

Oh, the frustration of it, she groaned inwardly, thinking of the skinny man in the Saint Laurent sheet, and dozens of others back in New York who were eager to jump on her bones.

Okay, she thought, reaching into the small crocheted shoulder bag she was wearing disco-style, angled down across her chest. No one could appeal to everyone. And it was friendship she wanted with Lew, not steamy passion. But the sort of friendship that would lead to marriage. Tender friendship. With physical intimacy, sure, because she was a normal human being, and she wouldn't want her marriage to be a sham. After glossing her lips to a shimmering pink, she dropped the makeup back into her bag.

A pretty good deal for some lucky man, she told herself, beginning to be indignant. Especially for a man who, like Lew, had had a romance turn inside out on him ... who ought to yearn for a simpler, safer connection.

She had the world's greatest daughter ... she was attractive ... she even had a rent stabilized Manhattan apartment!

Heading back to the action, ready to tell Lew just how silly she thought he was being, she was dismayed to see that Didi had arrived and Lew was dancing with her ... and James was sitting at the table.

As he rose to greet her, displaying his bedsheet in all its splendor, she couldn't keep her eyes from straying down his lanky torso toward his middle.

"Looking for something?" he asked urbanely.

"Oh, I was just admiring the authentic Greek garment around your waist." He'd cinched his toga with a preppy Brooks Brothers maroon and blue striped belt. "I thought I might want to get one like it for my brother."

"I didn't know you had a brother." Sipping from his mug of black velvet, he looked over the rim with that characteristic smug amusement in his clear gray eyes.

"Well, in case I have a brother someday," she said absurdly. As she sat down she couldn't help thinking that they fell into rhythm as naturally when they talked—even when they talked nonsense—as when they played tennis.

"Ah, yes." He sat his drink on the table and drew his chair closer to hers. "You're the woman who came to The Ladders to find a brother." Putting a casual arm around her shoulders, he added, "To answer your burning unspoken question—no, I'm not wearing what Mrs. Platt calls 'unders.' I was brought up to play by the rules." He gave her a comradely squeeze and let his hand drop, easing her mind but making her shoulder feel bereft.

"So. How's it going?" he asked.

She gestured glumly toward Lew and Didi. "Do you have to ask? Look at them, dancing sheet to sheet." She tasted her drink, then pushed it away. The ice had melted, leaving her with licorice-flavored water that was both cloying and thin.

"Sorry, pal. I did my best to help you."

"What do you mean, help me?" she echoed tartly. Craning to read the clock over the bar, she added, "You left me stranded here for forty minutes. What if Didi had showed up?"

He stared at her in astonishment, his mouth literally dropping open. "Isn't it dreadfully hard work?"

"Isn't what hard work?" Her impatience was mounting.

"Always striving to think the worst of me," he chided, waggling her nose. "The reason Didi didn't show up earlier is that I abducted her. I thought the whole point was to give you time alone with Lew."

Questions flew to her mind. Forty minutes . . . it couldn't have been much of an abduction. Still, the thought of him so much as kissing Didi in that special way of his, a tiger one moment and a lamb the next, tied her stomach up in knots. But she had no right to be jealous, she sternly reminded herself, even if she had reason. On the other, other, other hand . . . oh, heavens!

Her confusion turned to anger at him. He'd said he would help her get things going with Lew and make her life simple again, and he hadn't come through for her.

"Well, it was the wrong kind of time alone," she snapped.

As if to underscore her point, Lew and Didi danced past them, and he slid his hands down her back and held her in an undisguised embrace. They were a classic mismatch of a couple—Didi taller by a good three inches and decidedly flashier—but neither of them seemed to mind. They were laughing and chattering away. Even at a few yards distance, Carrie could tell they were having a grand time.

"Now, see here," James said, "it's not my fault if you didn't take advantage of the setup. What was I supposed to do—write your lines for you?"

Tipping his chair back and clasping his hands behind his head, he trilled, "Oh, Lew, your big, sweet, innocent brown eyes drive me out of my mind. They're like chocolate bars melting in the sun . . . like the mudpies of beautiful children at play . . ."

"Shut up," she said, but totally without venom. No other man had gotten her angry with such regularity . . . and no other man could so readily charm her out of her anger. "Help me! What am I going to do? Just when I thought the talk was getting good, he started in on braces and aphids. I think that's right where he'd like to stay with me."

"Well, then you've got to find some other way of getting your message across." Languidly unfolding his long body, he stood up and offered her a hand. "Let's dance."

She shook her head, fearing she'd be lost again if she moved around the floor in his embrace. "We tried making him jealous before, and it didn't work," she said. "Anyway, I told him you and I had decided to let things cool down."

"Give me a little credit. I wasn't going to repeat myself. We'll dance with perfect decorum, and after a few minutes we'll cut in on them. Once he's in your arms, he won't be able to resist you." He gave her a reassuring smile.

The music shifted to Gerry Mulligan's honeyed, tangy big-band rendition of "Moonlight in Vermont." As James swung her into the rhythm, his lime-and-clove scent invaded her nostrils, and it took all her self-control to keep from closing her eyes and laying her cheek against his wonderful chest.

Really, it wasn't fair that they moved around the dance floor as if they'd been designed to flow together. He was ten inches taller than she was. Her flat sandals did nothing to close the gap. She should feel like a chipmunk dancing with a giraffe. In reality, she felt more like Ginger Rogers dancing with Fred Astaire.

But, she told herself, no doubt every woman he'd ever danced with had felt right at home in his smooth and practiced clutches. Dozens of satisfied-goddess faces flashed across her mind, and her spine went rigid.

"Now, see here," he said, "when you dance with a fellow, you're not supposed to be going after the perfect posture award."

Irrationally, she felt offended. "I'm sorry," she huffed.

"Oh, it doesn't bother me," he said breezily. "I

was thinking about Lew." Gently urging her head toward his heart, he directed, "You want to cozy up. Like this. Then he'll be able to smell your fabulous perfume. Have I told you that one of the things I like about you is that I can't smell your perfume unless we're this close? So vanilla and edible— Shalimar, isn't it?" He buried his nose in her hair, humming.

There was no keeping her eyes open, or reality firmly fixed in her mind. For an exquisite moment, as they danced sublimely together, the two of them were all the world.

A fantasy took hold of her, and they were gliding because it was winter and they were skating, alone on a crystalline pond she remembered from her childhood, an island with silver birches and a gently arched bridge. And a flock of Canada geese who hadn't made it all the way south were arching their proud, long green necks and begging for bread crumbs. And it was night, and snow was falling, and the snow turned into stars, every snowflake a falling star, the wide black sky exploding with wishes, enough to fill a life. I wish . . . I wish . . .

"Thin ice! Thin ice!" called the geese.

Perhaps he heard them, too, and wanted to save her. Touching his lips to her forehead in the briefest of kisses, he said huskily, "I think we'd better cut in on Lew and Didi. Remember, cuddle up. It's obvious you're not going to get anywhere with this guy if you wait for him to make the moves."

"Hi, there," Lew said brightly as he surrendered Didi to James, not without a certain air of reluctance, and took Carrie gingerly into his arms.

"Hello, yourself," she purred. "It's nice to be your partner again."

Laughing nervously, he stepped on her foot.

"Maybe I better be captain this time too," Carrie said coyly. Nestling against him, she added, "Hold me a little tighter, and we won't trip over each other." He obeyed with a noticeable absence of fervor, and she leaned her cheek against his. "There. Doesn't that feel more natural?"

"Yes," he said weakly, pulling back.

"What's the matter, Defender? There isn't any Grotney L. Decay in my mouth, is there?"

He laughed. "No. Though did you ever stop and think—what's the technical term for decay?"

She thought for a minute, then groaned. "Oh, my gosh. Caries." Shaking her head, she asked, "Is that what comes to your mind every time you're near me? And to think that my mother always said a girl couldn't do better than to marry a dentist," she improvised hastily. "How come she gave me the one name practically guaranteed to turn off the whole profession?" She paused hopefully, waiting for him to say that no man in his right mind could be turned off by Carrie Delaney.

"Well, not the only name," he said enthusiastically. "She might have named you Ginger, which would make me think of gingivitis. That's an inflammation of the gums, if you've had the good luck not to need to know the term."

"Or she might have named me Cavafy, after the great Greek poet," Carrie couldn't resist saying. "And you know what else begins with c-a-v and ends with y." Laughing, she said, "We do have a good time together, don't we?" She lay her cheek against his.

He sneezed.

"Bless you!"

And again.

"Bless you! I hope you're not coming down with something. It's James who deserves to catch cold," she said heartlessly, "after his dunk in the stream."

Lew groped for a nonexistent pocket, and she dug a tissue out of her crocheted bag.

"Actually," he said sniffling, "I think it's an allergy. You're wearing Shalimar, aren't you?"

"You're allergic to Shalimar?" Pulling back, she saw that his eyes were red-rimmed. "I think you really are."

The invisible person in charge of the music—an eclectic, to say the least—filled the room with the beat of Michael Jackson. Palpably relieved to hold Carrie at arm's length, Lew began gyrating enthusiastically.

"Phyllis started wearing Shalimar after years of Madame Rochas," he said loudly, competing with the swelling music. "I thought it was the greatest stuff I'd ever smelled. Then it turned out that Matt had given her the first bottle, and instant allergy. The psyche's a wonderful thing, isn't it?"

"I'll never wear it again," she vowed.

"I didn't mean—" he began, looking around nervously. He all but whistled with joy when James and Didi, laughing conspiratorially, cut in.

"What have you two been finding so funny?" Carrie suspiciously asked her tall blond partner.

"I've been telling her knock-knock jokes." His fingers pressed tenderly into Carrie's back as he drew her into his rhythm. "Knock knock."

Carrie leaned against his chest, inhaling. "Who's there?"

"Toga."

"Toga who?" she asked, a giggle bubbling up to her lips.

"Together we can climb the highest mountain and swim the wildest river," James said.

Carrie groaned. "That's absolutely the worst knock-knock joke I've ever heard, and as a mother of a six-year-old, I've heard them all. Knock knock."

He pulled her closer, and her breasts pressed against him, seeking, yearning.

"Who's there?" he inquired gravely.

"Lew is allergic," she said, pretending her body was feeling nothing special at all.

"Lew is allergic who?"

"Lew is allergic to Shalimar. What am I supposed to do now?"

"Well, I could punch him in the nose," James

said helpfully, "and then he wouldn't be able to smell you."

"Thanks a lot." Goose bumps prickled her flesh; he was blowing softly into her hair. "I suppose I could go back to Zermatt and shower. But how on earth would I explain it to Dannie? I'm sure she's not asleep yet. It was disruptive enough last night when I went back to change for tennis."

"I've got it." James broke out of the dance and, hand on her wrist, led her toward the door.

"Where are we going?" Carrie demanded.

"The women's locker room. No one will be there at this hour." He steered her down a narrow corridor adorned with blue-green indoor-outdoor carpeting.

Carrie skidded to a halt. "Are you out of your mind?"

"Probably," he said calmly. Putting his hands on either side of her face, he said, "You make some men sneeze, and others you make craaazed with passion."

As his lips came down on hers, panic and desire twined together in her belly.

"Please—" she began with a little whimper. "We mustn't—" She kissed his lower lip. "Lew and Didi—" She kissed his upper lip. "Will be do-ing—" She kissed both corners. "Things like this."

James shook his head, projecting dismay. "You're right. We can't let that happen, can we?" He rapped on a metal door on which someone had cleverly stenciled JOCKETTES. Rattling the knob noisily, he pushed the door open and cheerfully called, "Knock knock."

"Who's there?" Carrie chirped nervously as he gently pushed her inside.

The tiled floor sloped downward to a central drain and still smelled of the day's quotient of chlorine. The rest of the room was equally salubrious, featuring a functional symmetry—two square white sinks, two mirrors in metal frames, two stall showers, two paper-towel dispensers. And two yearning bodies.

"Nobody but," James said, teasing her with his nearness.

She swallowed hard. "Nobody but whom?"

"'Whom!'" he echoed. "Always the English teacher! Nobody but us chickens, that's whom."

"Who," she corrected gently, floating into his arms as his mouth grew swollen in invitation.

His lips whispered across hers, then thundered, then whispered again, taking her from height to height, satisfying her as no simple sensation could have.

Oh, how cruelly unfair that so rich and gorgeous a feeling could lead one into total darkness! If Gar had aroused such sensations in her, would she have trusted in his goodness and the permanence of their love?

The instant the question was posed in her mind, she strained after it like a trout going for a minnow—but too late. It hung there neon-bright in her mind. How unbearable to acknowledge that full love-making with the man she had married, the man who had fathered her child, had pleasured her less than mere kisses with this near stranger.

In anguish she pulled herself back from his body and her own thoughts.

James ruffled her hair and sighed. "Never say I don't take you anywhere nice."

She smiled wanly, eliciting a puzzled look and then a shrug—as though to say he was growing used to being puzzled by her.

Moistening a paper towel, testing it for temperature and softness as if she were a baby, he said, "You smell so delicious, I can barely stand to do this. Tell me where you dabbed the dread Shalimar."

Silently she pointed to the pulse points at her throat and behind her ears. He tenderly rubbed with the wet paper towel, then sniffed the offending spots.

"That's better, then. Just a whiff of vanilla left, like the custard in a good trifle. But I've made you red with my rubbing." He bent and laved her with healing kisses.

She stood rigid under his ministrations, feeling that if she moved, she would weep.

"What's the matter, pal?"

She looked down, studying the green and white pattern in the tile. Two greens this way, then a white, and it reversed in the other direction.

"It's not fair," she whispered.

"What isn't?"

"Everything. Beginning with Gar being dead and ending with—Shalimar." She sniffed once, then forced a smile. "And I'm not being fair to you, getting all droopy. That wasn't part of our deal."

"I can take it," he said gravely. "I can take it all."

"Can you?" Scarcely knowing what she was doing, she said in a soft voice, "Then I have a confession to make."

"Yes?"

"I put a dab of perfume between my breasts."

He said nothing, but a muscle worked in his cheek, and she knew it had moved him to hear the word, as it had moved her to say it. With slow, deliberate motions, he spread the V of her toga, exposing the shallow valley and the pale, firm, round slopes on either side.

Wetting a fresh towel with warm water, he lifted her pearls out of the way and made a half dozen gentle up-and-down strokes. With a groan he threw away the towel and pressed his lips where his fingers had been.

Reeling, Carrie reached behind her and sought the support of the sink. A white light filled her vision. Oh, heavens, what angels, what demons had she unleashed?

"Carrie. Carrie." Standing at arm's length from her, he pierced her with his eyes, flashing a message of fiery desire.

She stood immobilized, knowing the slightest

movement would be taken for a nod of permission. She did want him so! And she must deny herself as well as him.

A single tear slid down her cheek. His hopeful expression deflating, he readjusted her sheet.

"That goes down in history as one of the all-time great displays of self-control," he said hoarsely. "Now, let's get out of this place before it's too late and I lose all my gold stars."

Pangs of guilt mingled with her shuddering regret. "I'm sorry," she whispered. "I had no right to do that. Forgive me. I didn't mean to be a tease."

"I know," he said on the tail of a sigh. He patted her on the head. "But I'm bloody well mad at me. This whole damned project was my doing. Frankly, the sooner you're Mrs. Lew Richards and safely off limits, the happier I'll be."

Moments later, back in Lew's arms, Carrie felt dizzy and nauseated, as skewed as a record being played at the wrong speed.

"Defender, I need air," she said.

"Sure." He seemed relieved to disconnect from her.

"I got rid of most of the Shalimar," she said, trying to distract her own mind with bright chatter. "When we're outside, you'll probably be able to bear being close to me."

They threaded their way around the plastic lounge chairs that surrounded the pool. The moon swung out from under a cloud. It had lost weight since the evening before, and looked wan but elegant. A silvery mist was climbing the side of the mountain.

"It's nice out here," Lew said.

"Yes."

He cleared his throat. "Do you feel better now?"

"I do." She desperately scrambled for clever words, but none came.

"Carrie—" He reached out and patted her arm.

"Yes?" She all but leaped at him. "Yes, Lew?"

He cleared his throat again. "I know you're not in love with me," he said. "Are you?"

She closed her eyes, then opened them. She sighed. "No."

"Then why—" He ran his hands through his hair. He swallowed. He cleared his throat again. "Why have you been coming on to me?"

She picked up a stick she saw lying on the ground and threw it as far as she could. "Because I'm not in love with you," she said.

They headed past the courts where they had played tennis. Though no one was playing now, the night lights were on, creating eerie white air.

"Frankly, I don't get it," Lew said.

"I told you, romance breaks the heart. I married a guy I was in love with, and when he died I thought I'd die, and I don't ever want to be that vulnerable again."

Staring at her fingers, she went on. "I figured you might feel the same way. Because your great love worked out the way it did. And I do like you, and Dannie adores you, and I thought maybe we could make . . . an arrangement. A marriage," she said defiantly, looking him straight in his big brown eyes. "I could tell from the way you looked at me at the cocktail party last night that you were sort of attracted to me. And I'd be good to you. You wouldn't be unhappy." The last words emerged in a rush as she sat down on the moon-washed grass.

Sitting down next to her, he put a friendly hand on her arm. "I'm very flattered. Maybe I shouldn't be," he added with a laugh, "but I am because I think you're a decent person, and I guess what you're saying is you think I'm one too."

He plucked a blade of grass, looked it over, and said, "I never could figure out how to make a grass whistle." Folding the blade, he put it to his lips and blew, but the only sound that came out was the hissing of his breath. "I bet James can make a grass whistle," he said. "It goes with knowing how to skip stones. I never had that knack either."

Carrie looked at his pleasant, relaxed face and took in the faintly wistful yet not at all bitter words. "You're more than decent. You're terrific," she said, meaning it.

"Hey, watch out," he answered lightly. "You might fall in love with me, and then where would you be?"

He leaned over suddenly and kissed her on the lips. His mouth was warm and sweet and tender against her mouth . . . and the kiss moved her not a jot.

"Tell me about how good you'd be to me," he said softly.

Flushing, she put her hands on either side of his face and kissed his nose, his cheeks, his chin. "There."

He took her hands in his and held them gently. "I think I should tell you two things," he said. "One is that when I first saw you last night, I thought you were the woman I'd come here to find. When James got you in his clutches I was seething because I'm always losing out to tall blond worldly men. Matt, for notable instance. The tennis confused the hell out of me at first, but then Didi and I started sending off sparks and, frankly, I no longer cared what game you and James were playing."

"We weren't playing against you—except at tennis," Carrie said, feelings of guilt welling up.

"Oh, I know that. He ruffled her hair reassuringly. "We both know that."

Drawing a breath, he went on, "The other thing I want you to know is this. Phyllis wasn't my great love. My great love was a red-haired belly dancer I met when I was in dental school. She'd been hired to jump out of a cake at my advisor's fiftieth birthday party. She really fell for me, too, but everyone went crazy—my parents, her agent, the dentist who was going to take me in as a junior partner. They all said we'd destroy each other. I ended up marrying the woman who had what the psychologists call the perfect profile for me—right age, right size, right religion, right profession—and she kicked me in the teeth. Some place to kick the dentist, huh?"

Smiling, he concluded, "You're nothing like Phyllis in character. You really are a lovely woman. But you're all those other 'rights.' And I was drawn to you because we tend to repeat our mistakes, as the psychologists also say. You would never have kicked me in the teeth, but you wouldn't have made my world go around any more than I would have set yours spinning. Didi's the one to do that for me. And James, I suspect, is the one to do it for you."

Looking earnestly at her, he said, "Aren't we lucky to have found them? And to have each other for friends?"

But she didn't feel lucky. She felt like a child whose big beautiful red balloon had burst. And the balloon man had gone away, and wouldn't be back until next year.

She told him she was deeply touched that he'd spoken his heart to her. And she wished him every kind of joy. And she was going back to her chalet to pack and would head home first thing in the morning.

CHAPTER FIVE

CARRIE LET HERSELF into Zermatt, then stood breathless in the foyer, a hand over her pounding heart.

Gretchen came padding out of the living room in her socks, a finger marking her place in the gossip magazine she'd been reading. She looked like someone who who'd been interrupted by unexpected and not entirely welcome company.

"Hi," she said, shifting her gum. "You're home early. Playing tennis again?"

"Not tonight I'm afraid. I have a headache." Taking in Gretchen's crestfallen expression, she added,

"But I want to pay you for a full evening."

"Oh, that's okay. Maybe Thursday or Friday you'll have a late night." Nodding encouragingly, she added, "That's the way it often works at these single-parent weeks."

"Well, that's not the way it's working for me," Carrie snapped. She took off her crocheted disco bag and wearily dropped it onto a bench piled high with tourist brochures. She knew Gretchen had meant no offense, but her words brought home the humiliating nature of this stay at The Ladders. "As a matter of fact," she added curtly, "we're cutting our trip short. I'm planning to leave tomorrow morning."

"Oh, no. Poor Dannie," Gretchen exclaimed. "She'll be so disappointed. Come on, I'll show you what I mean."

Beckoning Carrie toward Dannie's room, she stood back deferentially to give Carrie the view. There, on one of the twin beds, lay the elfin, dark-haired girl, beatific in the glow from the bathroom light, snoring softly—not under sheet and blankets but in her sleeping bag.

"She's so excited about the sleep-out tomorrow, she asked if she could have a pretend one tonight. I hope you don't mind." Gretchen anxiously fingered her pink sweat shirt. "And I let her read her good-night chapter by flashlight. I figured once wouldn't hurt her eyes."

"No, of course I don't mind," Carrie said softly. She tiptoed into the bedroom and tenderly kissed her daughter's smooth forehead.

"Oh, baby, baby," she murmured softly. "I'm sorry. I thought I had a nice daddy lined up for you." She knelt there for a moment, relishing her daughter's sweet breath; then Dannie stirred restlessly, her arms flailing, and Carrie got up and quietly hurried from the room to keep from waking her altogether.

Passing the open bathroom door, she caught sight of herself in the mirror. In her absurd draped sheet, she now looked less like a mythic Greek goddess than a tired Halloween ghost who'd been tricked instead of treated.

And she was giving up the ghost too easily, she suddenly thought, her self-pity turning to self-reproach. Was this what she'd meant by a do-or-die effort to find a decent life companion and a father for Dannie?

Really, Delaney, she scolded the pale woman in the mirror, you ought to feel ashamed, quitting after one little setback. Lew can't be the only fuzzy-wuzzy in the crowd, you know.

Out in the living room, Gretchen was busily gathering up Dannie's coloring books and crayons. Hearing Carrie come in, she gave the pile a final pat and crossed to the couch to collect her worn shoulder bag.

"I'm sorry if I was out of line, Mrs. Delaney," she mumbled. "About the late nights and everything."

"That's all right, Gretchen. I'm sorry if I jumped

on you. I'm afraid I lost my sense of humor at the toga party. You take very good care of Dannie, and to my way of thinking, that outweighs everything else. Not that there's much to outweigh," she added with a smile.

She went into her bedroom and returned with her wallet.

"I want to pay you for four hours," she said. "And maybe I was a little hasty about going back to New York. I do want Dannie to have the experience of a sleep-out. That's pretty exotic stuff for a city kid. And I did promise to take her to the Alpen Slide on Thursday. So let's keep our date for Thursday and Friday evenings. You'll look out for Dannie tomorrow night, won't you?"

Gretchen, along with the other regular baby-sitters at The Ladders, was slated to be a counselor on the fabled sleep-out.

"Of course I will. She's really special—very sweet, and about the smartest six-year-old I've ever seen. Oh, by the way"— Gretchen stuffed the dollar bills into the pockets of her snug-fitting jeans—"I hope that kid named Phillip isn't going on the sleep-out."

"I have no idea," Carrie said stiffly.

"Dannie really doesn't like him. She said that in the car today he told her he was going to throw up all over her."

Carrie ushered Gretchen toward the door. "That's not exactly what he said, but never mind. Thanks for telling me. Thanks for everything. Good night."

After turning out the living room lights Carrie went into her bedroom. As she stripped off her sheet and bashed it into the linen hamper, she vowed she would never again wear a toga. She would bob for apples . . . she would enter a greased-watermelon race . . . but no more togas.

Would she go skinny-dipping with strangers?

There was a "night swim au naturel" scheduled for tomorrow, when most of the children would be safely away from The Ladders on their sleep-out. She had imagined herself having a pleasant dinner with Lew, having finished with the ice-breaking games, but scratch that foolish dream.

Looking into the full-length mirror, she saw a body that many women would envy and many men would covet. Small-breasted, narrow-hipped, she couldn't claim to swell a bikini to mind-bending proportions, but she knew that, naked, she could hold her own in any crowd. She had the trim, sleek lines of someone who ate melon rather than sandwiches for lunch, who ran instead of walked. And she'd gone skinny-dipping as a child; she remembered the extraordinary sensation of being one with the water.

She would take part in the nude swim, she decided. If she felt uncomfortable, she could always leave.

If James were there . . .

A picture flashed into her mind, unbidden, unwanted. James, naked, poised on the diving board, his long pale body silvery in the moonlight, the epitome of animal grace.

Shaking her head, she turned away from the mirror to keep from being devoured by the hunger in her own eyes. She got the shower going full blast, punishingly hot and strong.

But the pummeling water only branded his name into her skin. James . . . James . . . James . . .

Somehow she'd been safe as long as a part of her had focused on Lew. Now her dangerous desire for the wickedly attractive Englishman was front and center in her mind, unchaperoned.

She'd been right; she should pack up their bags and take Dannie back to New York. But Dannie would be crushed to miss the sleep-out.

Lew had been a hopeless idea from the start, a ridiculous delusion, and any effort to make a match with another teddy bear would be similarly doomed. But that left her at the mercy of the slickies, the womanizers, the men who, like her father, would charm a woman to her destruction.

She could ask James not to come to the skinny-dip if he really had her interests at heart. But how hopelessly selfish of her even to consider asking, especially if Lew had wrapped up Didi.

She and Dannie were the world's greatest twosome, complete unto themselves. But single parents and only children sometimes grew unhealthily close. She and Dannie needed everything.

But, but, but...

On the other, other, other, other hand...

Toweling herself briskly, she put on her pale green robe, silk blended with a touch of acrylic. It had the sleekness and shimmer of the real thing without the wrinkles, and it unfailingly made her feel good about herself.

She stretched out on her bed and picked up a book, but no matter how she piled the pillows, she couldn't get comfortable for reading. Or maybe it was that the unoccupied half of the double bed was so yawningly, blatantly empty. She tried positioning herself dead center, only to feel as if she were adrift at sea.

"Delaney, you're getting neurotic," she muttered. She flung herself out of the inhospitable bed and went back out to the living room. Turning on a single lamp, she settled down on the motel-basic nubby beige couch opposite the fireplace, and made another stab at reading her book.

Wrong book though—one of Dorothy Sayers's mysteries starring the tall, blond, thin, oh-so-very-British upper-class detective, Lord Peter Wimsey.

And Harriet Vane, the slim, dark-haired heroine of the mystery series, fought off Peter's overtures through volume after volume until she finally married him. And there in a nutshell, Delaney, she told herself, is the difference between literature and life.

She fell asleep on the couch and woke, shivering, in the middle of the night. Stumbling back to bed, she thought Lord Peter was waiting for her, but cold sheets were her only companion.

She woke for good as the gray light of dawn edged her windows and the birds began chirping matins. Going to the kitchen and getting the coffeemaker started, she deliberately rattled and clattered, hoping to rouse Dannie. She couldn't stand being alone, listening to her own interior voices struggle to arrive at the rational conclusion that seemed to be within reach but kept eluding her. She desperately needed her child's innocent presence to purge her brain.

Hadn't Dannie always come through for her, even when she was a tiny infant? This morning she was more than ever her mother's boon companion, rising cheery and chattery, full of make-believe stories about her night of sleeping-bag bliss.

"And then the baby bear came over and cuddled up with me, and I wasn't the least bit scared because the wishing star fairy was there to keep me safe. And she looked just like you, Mama, except that she had wings, and she was wearing a turquoise lace gown. Would you wear a gown like that sometime?"

Carrie knelt to bestow hugs. "I'm not really the turquoise-lace type, sweetie. But I can tell you this— the wishing star fairy is always there to keep you safe."

"Will she be there tonight at the real sleep-out?" Dannie's voice trembled just a little.

"Absolutely," Carrie hastened to assure her. "You look up and find the Big Dipper and count two stars over to the left, and there she'll be. And even if it's cloudy and you can't see her, she'll see you." Brushing back Dannie's long silky hair and kissing her soft cheek, she said, "Let's have an early morning adventure. Breakfast out."

Dannie clapped her hands. "Hooray. Just like in the city. At a counter?"

The two of them often had breakfast out on a Saturday or Sunday, and Dannie cared less about the menu than about the presence of a counter with revolving stools.

"We'll see if we can find a counter," Carrie said. She stood up. "Last one dressed is a rotten egg."

"And first one dressed has to eat it!"

As they headed out toward the parking lot, identically garbed in faded denim overalls, pink T-shirts, and sneakers, Carrie cast covert looks toward the main building. A few early birds in tennis whites and running clothes were on their way into breakfast, but—thank heavens—no familiar faces were among them. She didn't know whom she was less eager to see, Lew or James.

James, she decided, with stomach-jarring certainty. Really, the whole humiliating debacle with Lew had been his fault.

Suddenly the unpleasant truth she'd been groping toward all night tumbled into place in the clear light of morning. To put it plain and simply, she'd been had. James had claimed they were playing a game together, but in fact he'd been playing a joke from the very beginning, and she'd been the butt of it. He'd probably barely managed to hold back his derisive laughter.

Oh, no Lord Peter Wimsey, he! Winding the reel back to the moment when she'd first seen him standing in the doorway of the cocktail lounge, she realized how devastatingly on target her first impression of him had been. The man was poison, and she'd made the catastrophic mistake of thinking she was immune to him when, in fact, she was as vulnerable as a babe.

Knock knock. Who's there? Eugene. Eugene who? You genius, Delaney, you really outsmarted yourself this time.

Oh, what she wouldn't give to buy back her kisses, to swallow the unwise words he'd tricked her into saying!

"Mom, you're hurting my hand," Dannie complained.

Carrie snapped back to the here and now. "Sorry, darling," she said contritely. She rubbed the little fingers. "We'll put my hand on the jerk list."

"Number sixty-three," Dannie said with something like glee.

Carrie had invented the jerk list a year ago to quell the tears that had poured out when Dannie had stumbled into a pothole on Fourteenth Street and painfully twisted her ankle. Privately she'd maintained her own grown-up jerk list, populated not by potholes and table corners and splinters and careless hands, but by the many men who'd disappointed her.

Hear ye, hear ye, let the infamous name of James Luddington be entered upon these rolls.

But driving down toward the Sugarbush access road, confronted by the relentlessly upright splendor of the mountains, she couldn't be less than completely honest with herself. And the bitter truth was, she belonged on the jerk list herself, for she'd been all too eager a co-conspirator in her own downfall.

She'd wanted an excuse, any excuse, to taste James's spicy kisses. She'd reveled, too, in their spicy verbal exchanges, and in their mutual delusion that they were different from—better than—the rest of the crowd at The Ladders.

She was twenty-nine, a mother, a teacher, a responsible citizen. And she'd behaved with the reckless disregard for reality appropriate to a hormone-flooded teenager.

"Mom, look! Horses!"

Carrie looked, grinning. Her city-bred daughter, born within walking distance of the Central Park Zoo, took llamas, polar bears, and capybaras in stride. But a pair of sluggish ponies in a corral merited breathless excitement.

So did a stack of "silver dollars" at Rosie and Al's Pancake Pantry on Route 100, never mind the absence of counter and stools. Lacing her plate with

amber syrup, Dannie enchanted the crowd of breakfast eaters by reading aloud the handwritten signs
that covered the wall.

"'Through these doors pass the finest folk in the
world, our customers,'" she recited as if the phrase
were boldly original and witty. "'If you have a com-
plaint tell us. If you have a compliment tell the
world.'"

Momentarily seeing life through her daughter's
eager, unspoiled eyes, Carrie even worked up enough
of an appetite to tuck away most of a huge blueberry
waffle—only to feel it turn to cement in her stomach
when a tall, thin, blond man who might have been
James's first cousin walked into the eatery.

Dreading the thought of facing James, she persuaded Dannie that it would be more interesting to
visit the pretty, polished town of Woodstock than
to take part in the junior tennis clinic being held
that morning at The Ladders. But Dannie was frankly
bored by the classic green in the middle of town
and the grand white colonial inn facing it. And Carrie
found herself unable to look at the renowned hos-
telry without imagining sharing a bed with James
and making the staid old rafters ring.

From Woodstock they went to Quechee, where
a transplanted Irish glassblower named Simon Pearce
had taken over an old red-brick woolen mill. Here
Dannie was fascinated by the spectacle of artisans
at work, and Carrie was again tormented. For the
riveting sight of glowing molten glass at the end of

a pontil iron reminded her all too graphically of the way James transformed her body into an infinitely malleable blob of liquid fire.

Finally, after a long string of encounters with James in her mind, it was five o'clock, and the overnight campers were assembling in the reception area at The Ladders. And there he was, as real as stone, in a blue oxford-cloth shirt with rolled-up sleeves and a pair of rumpled khaki pants.

Twenty children, their parents, and assorted counselors were milling about the small green-carpeted area, but for Carrie there was only one place to fix her eyes, try though she might to focus them somewhere—anywhere—else. Watching James help Phillip reroll his sleeping bag, his body taut with concentration, Carrie tried telling herself that he was any old father, neither angel nor demon, that she'd invented the James who'd haunted her all over Vermont that day. But he seemed to sense that she was there, and he looked up from his task to fix his damnably knowing eyes on her, a crooked grin tugging at the corners of his lips. And she realized that, if anything, she'd underestimated the Englishman's power to thrill her and hurt her.

Unfolding himself with that trademarked aristocratic laziness of his, he ambled over to her and Dannie, beaming a thousand rays of connection.

"I missed you today," he said with elaborate casualness. His posture, his slightly angled eyebrows, the way he inflected his words all made it clear he knew Carrie's absence from The Ladders had been a statement of her feelings about him.

Before Carrie could answer he pitched his next words at Dannie. "Did you have wonderful adventures? Did you see any purple cows?"

"That's silly," Dannie said, but there was more admiration than scorn in her voice, and Carrie quaked. Unworthily, she'd counted on her daughter's continued allergy to the Luddington males. Her relief was palpable when Dannie asked, with genuine disgust, "Is Phillip going on the sleep-out?"

"He is, indeed, and you know what?"

Dannie kicked at a speck of dust with one red-sneakered foot. "What?"

"I have a feeling," James said, "that you two are going to come home from the sleep-out very good friends."

Dannie looked up at Carrie, her expression what it might have been had he announced that there would be brontosaurus sandwiches for supper.

Feeling put in the middle—she didn't, after all, really want to encourage Dannie in unjustified hostility to decent-enough small boys—Carrie said through clenched teeth, "That would be nice, wouldn't it?"

"Maybe," Dannie allowed grudgingly, and James laughed and waggled her nose the way he liked to waggle Carrie's.

"You two are related, all right," he said.

"Of course we are. She's my mother and I'm her

daughter." Dannie grabbed Carrie's blue-jeaned thigh, her statement of the obvious and her gesture tantamount to a declaration that she didn't like the grown-ups' behavior.

Carrie hoisted and hugged her, partly to reassure Dannie, partly to erect a screen between James and herself. Fortunately, the head counselor for the sleep-out—a freckle-faced, gung-ho assistant tennis pro named Bert Magruder, whom Dannie knew and liked from the tennis clinic the day before—picked that moment to blow the silver whistle he wore on a lanyard.

"Five minutes to a blast-off," he called cheerfully.

Pandemonium broke loose. While some kids were vocalizing their eagerness to get going, others were flinging themselves on their parents, begging not to be sent out into the unknown. Phillip came running over to James and mumbled something about needing to "spend a penny," and the Luddington males made a beeline for the men's room. Dannie simply got very quiet but brightened when Gretchen came in from the parking lot, where she'd been loading supplies onto the bus, and gave her a big hello.

Fighting her own anxieties about their separation, Carrie knelt down for a hug.

"Give my love to the wishing star fairy," she whispered lightly. "Tell her my wish is for you to have a fabulous night."

"And my wish is for you to have a fabulous

night," Dannie said with innocent fervor, bringing a blush to her mother's cheek. Then, giving a brave little wave, she grabbed her sleeping bag with one hand and Gretchen with the other and skipped out the door.

Looking out the window as the bus pulled away, her stomach tightening as she fretted about faulty seat belts, snakebites, and a thousand and one disasters that might possibly befall Dannie, Carrie was taken by surprise when a hand descended lightly on her shoulder.

"Don't worry, Mama," James's voice said in her ear. "She'll do just fine. Phillip's an old hand at camping, and I charged him to look after her or else, and never mind their little differences."

"Oh, terrific," Carrie drawled sarcastically. "There's nothing like being taken care of by a Luddington." Looking up at him, she glared angrily, then deliberately turned her head away.

She couldn't have made her feelings more obvious if she'd declared them in neon, but predictably—maddeningly—he refused to be riled.

"I do believe you're trying to tell me something." His tone was as light as popcorn. "You don't like my shirt?"

"Your shirt is too good for you." She folded her arms across her chest. "It's a gentleman's shirt."

"I see. Well, the last thing I want to do is misrepresent myself. I'll run right home and change into something more appropriate for a scoundrel.

Maybe a punk T-shirt with holes and a safety pin?"

She refused to look at him, but she knew how his gray eyes were twinkling. The conniver was having a wonderful time.

Meanwhile, life was going on around them, mercifully indifferent. A hand-holding couple in tennis clothes over at the reception desk were asking the portly, blow-dried assistant manager if they couldn't give up one of their chalets and share accommodations for the rest of the week—with a prorated refund; and the assistant manager was unctuously explaining that such adjustments were against The Ladders' policy. But if they got married, he cheerfully reminded them as he reached for a ringing phone, they would be entitled to a Gratis Anniversary Weekend Celebration a year hence.

"Of course, in all the best French films," James rattled on, "the devil wears a dinner jacket, so maybe what I need to do is dress up, not down. Alas, I didn't pack formal clothes, even though Mrs. Platt urged me to. 'You never know,' she said, and indeed you never do." Putting his fingertips on Carrie's arm, he added, "Will you have dinner with me this evening, despite my regrettable sartorial lapse? There's a place up the road called The Phoenix. I hear they have a way with duck, and the desserts are legendary."

Carrie yanked her arm away. "I wouldn't have dinner with you if you—"

"Got down on my knees and begged?" James's

golden eyebrows angled upward. "Well, I won't do that, don't worry. I'm saving the gesture for a more important moment. That Gratis Anniversary Weekend Celebration is a real inducement to do the right thing, isn't it? Give me credit though. I seem to remember proposing moments after I met you, and I swear I didn't know what the management was offering. Frankly," he went on as the phrase "rip-off" reverberated from the reception desk, "I don't think those two are going to make it through the week, much less to an anniversary. But they deserve each other, don't they?"

Numbed by his verbal onslaught, Carrie stared woodenly at him, wondering what devious turn his deceptively foolish words would take next. His gray eyes flickered, and in a flash the amusement drained from his face.

"You're hurting," he said, his voice incredulous. "Because a man who isn't remotely a match for you had the good sense to know it? I saw Lew and Didi looking pretty cozy today, and I figured that had something to do with your absence, but I was sure a day's mulling would help you see things in perspective. You mustn't feel scorned, my darling. Surely you knew from the start what our game was about."

"You set me up," she said tensely. "I rejected you—almost inconceivable that a woman could turn down someone with your charms, but I managed—and you decided you wanted the fun of seeing someone reject me."

He simply burst into laughter and tugged at her arm. "After a mouthful like that, you must be desperate for a chaser. Come on, I'll buy you a drink."

"I'm not playing anymore!" she shouted, coloring hotly as the assistant manager and the would-be chaletmates turned around and stared.

"Aren't you?" he countered quietly. "The centuries-old game of self-delusion?" He seemed to draw himself up to even greater than his usual height, the better to look down at her. "Why don't you admit what you really are, Carrie? And what you really want?"

She forced a smile to her lips. "Oh, I have no trouble admitting to that," she said. Gathering all her courage for a final riposte, she went on. "Come to the skinny-dip tonight, my darling, and you'll see exactly what I am and what I want."

Her lips began to tremble, and she turned quickly away, not wanting to spoil the effect of her needling words. But she had time to glimpse the dismay on James's face, and as she hurried out into the parking lot, it required all her self-control not to look back for another soul-satisfying glance at his expression.

Returning to a thunderingly empty Zermatt, she invented a dozen tasks to keep from thinking about the tall blond man she detested and the daunting prospect of swimming in nothing but her skin. She baked Dannie's favorite double-chocolate brownies. She ironed a white cotton skirt of her own and a rainbow-striped sundress of Dannie's, neither of which were truly wrinkled. She gathered up the tourist brochures she'd amassed and arranged them in alphabetical order. She persuaded herself she was hungry—more to fill time than to fill her tight belly.

After forcing down a few bites of a string bean and tomato salad and a handful of wholewheat crackers, she took her third shower of the day. Glancing at her traveling alarm clock, she discovered to her dismay that it was only eight-fifteen. The swim au naturel wasn't scheduled to begin until nine, when presumably any kiddies who hadn't gone on the sleep-out would be safely stowed away in their beds.

After painting her fingernails a fruity pink to match her toenails, she decided the effect was tacky and carefully removed every speck of polish. That endeavor at least had the benefit of chewing up twenty minutes, and at last it was time to head for the pool.

"It's perfectly okay to do this . . . you're a grown-up now . . . the naked human body is just another part of the natural world," she recited under her breath, pulling on a hooded red terry-cloth robe over nothing whatsoever. But she avoided all mirrors as she pulled the sash tight at her waist and double-knotted it while slipping her feet into red and white thongs.

Deciding to travel light, she dropped her key into one pocket of the robe and a tissue into the other. The management would provide towels. The only thing she needed now was a final dose of courage to get her out the door.

"A daddy for Dannie, a daddy for Dannie," she repeated. The words magically propelled her into the night and down the pine-scented hill.

The air was warmer than she'd expected, and as she looked up at the diamond-studded black velvet of the sky, she began thinking she might actually have a good time. Judging from the laughter and giddy shouts coming from the pool, a number of people already were having a good time.

Drawing closer, she saw that the management had shown unexpected good taste. Aside from the muted silvery radiance provided by the stars, the only lights in use were dim underwater spots, which safely illuminated the boundaries of the pool while politely obscuring the details of flesh.

She was relieved to see that Lew and Didi were nowhere in sight. She guessed that all the couples who'd already been formed were off making private whoopee.

Standing on the farthest edge of the lounge area surrounding the pool, she watched as an athletic-looking woman with a long tangle of blond curls did a perfect jackknife off the diving board, earning applause and whistles from a group of men. One of them caught Carrie's eye and beckoned to her, and she realized with a start of amusement and distaste that he was the man who'd stood arguing at the reception desk. There was no sign of the woman whose hand he'd been fervently clutching only hours ago.

She knew he wasn't the kind and cuddly mate

she was looking for, but if she stood on the edge of the crowd much longer, she was going to be more conspicuous than if she took off her robe and played the skin game. She had started untying her sash with suddenly clumsy fingers when a tall, thin figure unfolded from a shadowy chaise.

"No," James said. Wearing a classic black-watch tartan robe made of Vyella, he loomed over her. "You can't do this."

"No?" she echoed mockingly. "Did my mother send you?" She got one of the knots undone.

His eyes glittered like flashing knife blades. "You're doing this just to get back at me. Because you think—mistakenly—that I did you wrong."

"'Done me wrong,'" Carrie said, a bubble of a giggle bursting on her lips. "That's the idiom. You done me wrong. Of course, it hardly goes with the perfect Oxford inflection."

"Cambridge, actually, but who's counting."

As she got her sash undone he grabbed at the lapels of her robe to keep it together. Her skin sang and sizzled where his fingers made contact, and she had to struggle not to moan.

"I thought you were so eager to see my body," she mocked. Keep talking, Delaney, say anything; just keep talking. "I promise you, you won't be disappointed."

"Shut up," he said tersely. "Eager as I am to see every inch of you, I'm equally disinclined to share that privilege with this collection of horse's asses."

"Kowabunga!" A naked man threw a naked woman into the pool, then jumped in after her, their raucous laughter rhyming with the splashes.

"Point made?" James asked as Carrie struggled ineffectually to loosen his grip on her.

"I do believe we're losing our fabulous British sense of humor," she trilled. She finally ripped her robe open, only to have him clutch her in a tight embrace, sheltering her body from the world.

"Carrie, don't fight me," he pleaded, his lips feathering her cheeks, her earlobes, her eyelids, her chin. "Don't fight yourself. I love you. And I think you love me. You're a woman with the courage to struggle against everything that's false and evil in this life, but why fight what's good and beautiful and true? I'll make you happy, I promise. Dannie too. We'll all be happy together. It's meant to be."

Swooning as the gorgeous, insidious words swirled around her, Carrie went limp against his body, pressing helpless little kisses into the thrilling angles of his collarbones.

She no longer had the strength to fight him—least of all with the hungry crowd waiting to eat her up if she managed to break free. Let her body have its desire for one night. Let her heart dally ever so briefly in a fool's paradise.

"I want to go skinny-dipping," she murmured brokenly with a child's absurd stubbornness, making one last effort to keep from going over the edge.

"Then I shall take you skinny-dipping," he declared. He held her tight against him, his cheek pressed into her hair, his hands painting circles on her back. "In private. We'll go be babes in the woods, skinny-dipping the way the good Lord meant it to be. But it will be coolish," he went on, his voice matter-of-fact, "so we'll need sweaters and jeans and blankets and brandy and all that. Meet you at my car in fifteen minutes?"

Running back to her chalet, she felt like a puppet on a string. He had let her go, but he was controlling her every movement. The act of impulsively tossing a half dozen brownies into a plastic bag seemed a solitary sign of free will.

Yet her unaccustomed submissiveness was not unpleasant, even though it tasted like doom. At last she was released from the burden of thinking, weighing, deciding. Whatever would be would be.

He was waiting when she got to the car, but he didn't look worried; he had plainly known she would appear. Silent, smiling gravely, he opened the door of the Renault and ceremoniously guided her inside.

As they drove along the dark, curving roads of the mountain basin, the talk was desultory, impersonal, jumping from politics to sweet corn to soaring in gliders (a favorite sport on the Sugarbush ridge) to the strengths and weaknesses of various detective series (she omitted mention of the books starring Lord Peter Wimsey). They sat close to each other, using up a fraction of the space in the silver station wagon, and while they idled in front of a traffic signal at a deserted intersection, he tenderly kissed her.

She didn't ask where he was taking her. She guessed it was to the spot where they'd picnicked with Dannie and Phillip and Lew and Didi. When he took a right-hand turn off Route 100, she knew she'd guessed right.

As he pulled the car to a stop and turned off the engine, the roar of the waterfall filled her ears with an other-worldly music. Suddenly eager to get on with the unraveling of fate, she gave James a brief conspiratorial look, then bounded out to behold a magical scene.

Bathed in the eerie light from the thick sprinkling of stars and the fractional moon, the pool at the base of the falls gave off the trembling, anticipatory air of an enchanted pond. The pine and spruce, swaying slightly in the gentle breeze, were surely mythic spirits in disguise. Had a unicorn pranced out to drink from the sparkling water, she wouldn't have been surprised.

James produced a silver flask in a leather holster.

"I'm all right," she said, thinking he was offering liquid courage. Matter-of-factly, she began to unfasten her jeans.

He laughed. "I never doubted it. This isn't for your psyche. It's to give your thermostat a boost. There's no chlorine in this pool, but there isn't any heater either."

Taking a single swallow of the mellow brandy,

she said boldly, "Napoleon cognac, I bet. A hundred dollars the bottle. But you could have saved your money. Your kisses do exactly the same thing to my knees."

"Oh, brazen woman. Let's see what a combination of the two intoxicants can do."

After sipping from the flask he pressed his lips against hers. As his tongue probed, demanding entry, a bit of the brandy slid into her mouth, excitingly warmed, its bouquet enhanced by an extra perfume that was ineffably James.

Lord . . . it was as though he'd shared some precious bodily essence with her, their primal cells mingling. Sucking every exquisite drop into her own being, she felt his arms become her legs, his head her heart, and all known boundaries of the universe dissolved.

"If ever I needed cold water, it's now," she gasped. In one fluid motion she stripped off sweater, jeans, panties, and sandals.

Standing before him for an instant, she allowed herself the satisfaction of hearing him groan with desire.

"I knew you were beautiful, but I didn't know you were perfect," he said huskily. His eyes narrowing, he raised a hand to touch her, then stood still in motionless homage, saying her name again and again, the slow, disbelieving shakes of his blond head telling her he could hardly believe his good fortune.

As he started to unbutton his shirt, she ran down the path, the summer air a benediction on her skin. Breeze, stones, twigs, trees—all were her sisters. Nature had made her, and nature had summoned her here, to home.

Scarcely aware that James had shed his clothes and was coming down the path behind her, she ran into the shallow pool at the base of the falls. Despite the warming magic of the cognac, the water nipped and stung her ankles, and she remembered from childhood that the only antidote was immediate, total immersion in the water.

Moving gingerly over the smooth but not exactly welcoming stones that formed the stream bed, she found herself knee-deep, then mid-thigh deep. Giggling and shrieking at once, she grabbed her ankles and pulled herself downward until she was submerged to her shoulders.

Suddenly she was almost warm, flooded with a sense of fabulous well-being, and she threw back her head to look at the star-strung sky. James's moon-bright face floated over her. Embracing her from behind, he led her in a watery, weightless dance.

"Wood nymph. Enchantress," he accused her, his lips grazing hers as he swirled her through the water. "What chance does a mere mortal stand against you? Be merciful with me, I beg you."

Mimicking his favorite gesture, she reached up and waggled his nose. "No mercy for you, wicked man." She nipped his lower lip with her teeth. "You have many transgressions to pay for. Many, many transgressions."

"Tell me," he pleaded, "and have done with it." Turning her, he held her body against his.

"First, you made me—" Her voice wavered as her sensitized skin read his secret contours. "Want you," she managed to say, delivering another punishing nip. "And then, you made me—" Gasping, all but sobbing, she was suddenly seized by shivers that made her feel her flesh might disintegrate at any minute. "You made me—"

Scooping her up as though she were Dannie's size, he bounded out of the water and set her down on the bank. With complete disregard for his own dripping, shaking body, he grabbed two big towels and began vigorously massaging her fore and aft.

As her blood began to circulate and the shuddering subsided, she suddenly became acutely aware that both of them were naked. Watching her eyes take their fill of him, he shook an admonishing finger at her.

"Remember," he began in a teasing voice, toweling his legs with languid motions, "cold water may be just the thing to wash your woolen sweaters in if you don't want them to shrink, but it has exactly the opposite effect on the male anatomy. However, a beloved woman's warm hand—"

Breaking off abruptly, he clutched her to him, encircling her with his strong arms. "Say the words, Esmerelda. Tell me what I made you feel. First I made you want me, and then I made you—what, darling? Does it have four letters? Does it begin with *L?*"

Oh, heavens, how fantastic he felt, and how threatening he still was! A thousand clanging voices in her head cried out: Hold back! Hold back!

"Yes, Harold," she whispered into his skin, "a four-letter word beginning with *L*. L-i-k-e."

Spanking her very available bottom, he groaned, "Oh, you witch, Esmerelda. What do I have to do to hear what I want to hear?"

"Remember," she began, "you must seek the advice of the oracle on the mountain, or you will never pass the test." Then, unable to play another moment, she looked at him with beseeching eyes. "Please," she begged him in earnest, "please, James, let's have what we can have, and not—" Cold overcame her again, tearing at her with vibrations that she felt in every bone, and she burrowed into his chest, seeking an opening to swallow her and shelter her forever.

Again he scooped her up. "A sleeping bag. Brandy. Me," he pronounced, loping back to the car.

The next thing she knew, he was pulling something shapeless and mud colored out of the car, tossing it onto the soft grass on the far side of the infamous picnic table, unrolling and unzipping it, shoveling her into it, and following *tout de suite*. As he yanked the zipper closed and took her in his arms, she felt a surge of warmth worthy of a tropical sun.

"Smells a little bit musty," he said, "but it's a hundred percent down. It would keep you warm on Everest."

"If only you came with it." She snuggled into him, grateful for the small talk, the reprieve from the monumental inevitability soon to swallow her up. "How does someone so lean generate so much heat?"

"It's your inspiring presence." Pillowing her head with his arm, he offered her a sip from the flask.

Fortified, she inched her way upward out of her downy cocoon. As the luminous splendor of the infinite sky filled her vision, she gasped with pleasure. "I haven't camped out in fifteen years. I'd forgotten how different the stars look when you see them from this angle. Oh, James, quick, up there!"

A star had torn loose from its moorings and came streaking across the sky like a Fourth of July roman candle.

"I do hope the kids saw that," she said, her voice a little wistful.

He squeezed her reassuringly. "You're granted one hope per star, Mama. And one wish." His silver eyes outshone all the other stars as he propped himself up on an elbow and gazed down at her. "What's your wish, my lovely Carrie?"

With all the firmament to chose from, she met his eyes and blurted out, "Kiss me."

He was smiling smugly, but he'd earned the smugness, and she didn't mind at all. She felt the dear, quirky curve of his mouth as he brought his lips down to hers, at first just barely brushing the skin with a tantalizing lightness, then pressing home as though he wanted their very atoms to fuse.

Her hands in his hair, she answered his fervor with a frantic hunger of her own, her mouth moving incessantly lest it leave any millimeter of his lips untouched.

"Dearest," he said huskily, "how can it be that you seem so familiar to me? And yet I know that in fifty years you'll still taste brand new?"

A shudder seized her again, sponsored not by the cold this time but by his words. There could be no future for them, and he had to know it as well as she did. That fact wouldn't really be sad as long as they didn't lie to themselves and each other.

"Please—" she began, and he seemed to know what she was asking, for his kisses turned soft and contrite, moving from her mouth to her nose and her eyelids, a myriad of butterfly messengers whispering "Trust me" as they caressed her with their wings.

Another star streaked across the sky, commanding their attention, and if she hadn't known that the third week in August was prime time in Vermont for viewing falling heavenly bodies, she might have thought the world was coming to an end. But, oh, if it had to end, this was the way to go, with the exquisite quaking at the center of her body no less an event than the imploding sky.

"My turn to hope and wish," James said in her ear, his tongue languidly underscoring the words. "But I can't have you bounding from this bag like a frightened doe." She could feel his mouth curve into a smile as he added, "Besides, I can't wait another minute, my luscious little witch. Let's make . . . like."

His hands deserted her back to play on the soft silk of her throat and the pulsing hollows of her upper chest. Then they slid all at once to encompass the yearning hills of her breasts. Her nipples were torpid buds released by a sudden springtime, and as they burst into feverish flower against his palms, he emitted a musical sigh of triumph and desire.

As their lips bonded, and their tongues leaped to dance around each other, her hands began to have their own cravings. Shy at first, then emboldened beyond belief by his welcoming sounds and moves, she staked her claim to shoulders and elbows. She went gardening in the soft tangle of his chest hair. She teased his ticklish nipples. She memorized the whorls of his navel.

"Don't stop now," he said, commanding and pleading at once; and she willingly gave in to his aching need and her own.

His hands slid down over her flat belly, matching her intimate explorations of his body with a thrilling serenade of loving caresses, his fingers answering her every sweet ache and urging her on to yet more exalted desires.

Somehow he managed to shift them around in their cocoon, and he gathered her under him, his body as real as the sky and the mountains, yet somehow weightless.

"Welcome home," she whispered, gasping as he entered her.

"Carrie, Carrie, darling, dearest..."

Then the moment for words was past as they connected on the plain where essence speaks directly to essence, and all is understood.

The world had never seemed smaller or more infinite to Carrie, beginning and ending with this man; yet this man was everything. Thrusting, cruising, pumping, coasting—he made their sleeping bag a rocket ship, its destination the wildest, most inviting reaches of star-spangled outer space.

All too soon—yet not a moment too soon—they were two more brilliant explosions, achieving their ultimate glory as they flew into a billion fragments in synchronous apocalypse.

As the bits and pieces of their being reassembled, James shifted their bodies once more, spooning her against him. Sighing into her hair, clasping her for dear life, he said, "Tell me it was everything for you that it was for me."

"You know it was." She pressed kisses into his hands.

"Are you ever going to forgive me for making

you fall in love with me?"

"Please—" she began, the usual litany of protests rising through the layers of satiation in her brain.

But this time he would have none of it.

"Carrie Delaney, I love you. And I know you love me. And the time has bloody well come for me to collect my stellar hope and wish."

Defying the laws of the physical universe, he rose and compressed all at once until, by any definition, he was kneeling.

"The object of this posture is to place the supplicant below, not above, the revered one," he said, his customary jauntiness offset by a certain tremulousness. "But let's not quibble about details."

As she looked at him in open-mouthed numbness, he went on. "This is no joke, my darling—not that I was ever joking, even when I thought I was. For the third—or is it the fourth and I hope with all my heart it's the last—time: I want to spend my life with you, I want our kids to grow up as brother and sister. Carrie, most cherished of women, will you marry me?"

CHAPTER SIX

"JAMES. JAMES." RAISING her fingertips to his cheeks, she got the words out around a lump in her throat the size of a canteloupe. "You've made me love you, I admit that you've made me love you, but I can't marry you."

For a moment his face was sculptural in its stillness, then one corner of his mouth turned up in a derisive grin.

"*But* you can't marry me," he said in quiet mockery. "*But*. I think, Madame English Teacher, that you've got your conjunctions confused. What you mean is that you love me and *therefore* you can't marry me."

As graceful as if he'd been sauntering across a drawing room, he eased out of his absurd position and lay next to her, propped up on one elbow.

"I suppose the exalted passage we just shared was the final straw," he went on. "First I made your heart sing as it had never sung before, and then I made your body dance as you had never known it could. And if that doesn't make me the very definition of a rotter, I don't know what would. Forgive me," he wound up, "for insulting you by suggesting you align yourself with such a person."

Twin tears slid down her face. "Why did you have to spoil everything?"

"Spoil everything!" His laughter was a hollow, ringing bark. "My God, but we have come full circle since the days of Queen Victoria! That was the epithet usually flung at the poor fellow who was boor enough to follow a proposal of marriage with the chastest of kisses. 'Oh, Sir James,'" he piped in the pale, constricted voice of the Victorian maiden, "'how could you have done that? You've gone and spoiled everything!' Now, apparently," he went on in his own grating baritone, "it's undignified to propose marriage following what was obviously, for one of the participants, a mere athletic event."

"Oh, James, please," she began. "You know it wasn't any such thing for me. You just said so yourself. It's true, you have made my heart sing and my body dance, and I wish life were simple and I could think about the singing and dancing only and say yes to you."

"My dear love..." Shifting once more, he took her into his arms and held her close.

Feeling infinitely sheltered, she relished the sweet wind that brushed over her cheeks. The roaring of the falls and the rustling of the pines filled her mind. She longed to close her eyes and go to sleep and wake up in a world where there were no decisions to make.

But James would allow her no such peace.

"My dear love," he began again, "life *is* simple. Brutally simple. We're born, and in the blink of an eye we die, and in between, if we're very lucky, two great things happen: We find people to love who love us, and we find good work to do in the world. And if we're exceedingly lucky, the love and the work dovetail, and then we've really got it made."

In her eagerness to jump on his words she sat bolt upright.

"Yes, exactly!" she exclaimed. "That's one of the things I was going to say. How in the world can we marry if you have to live in New Hampshire and I have to live in New York?"

"Do you? Have to?" He pulled her back down into snuggling position.

"I really do. For one thing, Dannie's in the best school in the entire country for gifted kids. I mean, being at Hunter is like winning the lottery, that's what all the parents say. And I'm really committed to teaching in the New York City school system.

But really," she emphasized eagerly, her words tumbling over one another like drops over the falls, "too many good people are bailing out, and the very idea of public education in on the line, and I don't think I could live with myself if I walked out now. And, don't take this the wrong way, please, James," she went on, "but in a sense Gar died for New York. The least I can do is be there to bear witness."

She steeled herself, waiting for his derisive laughter, his mocking insistence that she had no idea what truly mattered in life.

She should have known better, she realized an instant later. She should have realized that the wily man in whose arms she lay would never have brought up the thorny matter of geography, or any other subject, except to turn the talk to his own advantage.

For he was positively crowing. "Darling! I'm so relieved to hear that you haven't secretly been longing for a life in the country. I've arranged, you see, to move to Manhattan. Because someone was telling me—I can't for the life of me remember whom—"

"Who," she corrected numbly.

"Who?"

"Because you're really saying, 'I can't for the life of me remember *who* was telling me'."

"But I remember perfectly!" James said gaily. "The most marvelous woman whom, whom, whom I ever met. And she said to me, she said, 'You're too tall and slick and generally superb a human being to live anywhere but among the soaring towers of Gotham. I must have you near me among the steel and angles and upthrust.' And that did it. I knew then and there that I could no longer live among the ovoid red beans of Boston or the green and white triangular mountains of New Hampshire."

"Heaven help me, I'll never utter another architectural metaphor as long as I live," Carrie cried to the starry vastness. Gently prying his hand from her breast, she brought it to her mouth and chastised it with her teeth. "'And that,' the woman in question said, 'is to give my words some non-metaphorical teeth.'" Then, suddenly suspicious that this supreme trickster had been putting her on again, hoping ever so strongly that he had been putting her on, she added confidently, "But you're joking, of course. Ever the joker."

"I'd like that hand back, if you don't mind. It was very happy where it was." Cupping her breast once more, he said, "If you think I'm kidding, my darling, you only have to read tomorrow morning's *New York Times.*"

The New York Times indeed! Feeling a wave of relief sweep over her, she snuggled closer to her utterly impossible but undeniably delicious bagmate.

"Uh-huh," she said. "A banner headline on page one—I can see it now. Luddington Moves to Manhattan—Washington and Kremlin Analyze Computer Programmer's Change of Jobs."

"Oh, dear." James nuzzled the back of her neck. "Did I tell you I was a computer programmer?"

"You certainly did," she began indignantly. Then, recalling their exchange of personal facts—had it been only two nights ago?—she amended, "I guess what you said was you got brought over to the States because you had a knack with computers." Feeling oddly disappointed, and chagrined at feeling anything at all, she said, "You're—what? In sales, then? Or what do they call it, hardware? Forgive me if I don't have the vocabulary right. I've deliberately remained computer-illiterate, to use the ridiculous phrase."

For a moment he didn't say anything, and she had the feeling he was weighing his words. But was it possible? James, who was always ready with the quip, the barb, the poetry-coated bombshell?

"Actually," he was saying diffidently, "I dreamed up the first really affordable home computer. So my move to Boston was more a matter of my going binational than a matter of being hired for a job. And though my impending move to New York won't be page one in the *Times*," he went on in the same matter-of-fact voice, "I do rather expect I'll be the lead story in the business section."

Carrie maneuvered one hundred eighty degrees to stare him in the face. But the beloved, incensing smile, the silver-and-steel eyes she suddenly knew better than her own, the falling blond lock he kept pushing back—none of it helped counterbalance the overwhelming sense of swirling unreality she felt at the moment.

Though she had a bias against computers, she lived in the modern world, and she had a daughter whose first grade class got an hour of computer lab every week, and—oh, heavens—the machine that Dannie prattled so fondly about at supper on Thursdays was called the Lud!

All at once, snatches of magazine articles glimpsed while waiting for Bernardo to cut her hair flew into her mind and assembled, a giant puzzle that was no less mystifying for being solved.

"You're one of the wonders of modern Britain!" she gasped. "Like Freddie Laker—and, good Lord, it's *Sir* Freddie and it really is *Sir* James, too, isn't it? My knight in shining armor!"

If she hadn't been flat on the ground to begin with, she probably would have ended up in that position, so violently did she giggle.

"What a dodo you must have taken me for!" she howled. "James Luddington . . . a knack for computers . . ."

"Well, I'm not exactly a household word," he said modestly. "Not on this side of the drink, anyway. Give me two years in New York, though, and even the English teachers are going to have to admit I exist."

Breathing as fast as if she'd run up Sugarbush Mountain, she lay on her back, a hand over her heart, staring up at the stars, trying to find her center again, her place in this brand new universe.

She knew he was telling her the truth, and yet it couldn't be the truth; she wasn't ready for such a truth.

"But you couldn't have. When did you talk to a *Times* reporter?" she asked, grasping at a hope, as though catching him in any inconsistency might be enough to make his whole story rewrite itself.

"Think, my darling—mother of Dannie Delaney, renowned detective." As she shook her head, bewildered, he went on. "It was your doing, really. Sending me into the arms of a reporter."

"You mean Didi? But she's on the staff of *The Hartford Courant*." Carrie's voice sounded shrill and hollow to her own ears.

"Yes, and what's her big wish?"

Carrie bit her lip. "To be a *Times* reporter by age forty."

"Exactly. And remember I told you I'd grant her biggest wish, whatever it was, to give you a little time alone with Lew? I hope I never really know what you thought she and I were doing when we absconded from the toga romp, but her interest in coming up with a story that would make the *Times* notice her coincided very nicely with my interest in letting you know, in bold type, that I was serious enough about you to move the headquarters of Luddington Bri-Merica to New York, and the tax situation be damned."

Her mouth flying open, she remembered the looks

of conspiratorial amusement James and Didi had shared at the toga party.

"Knock-knock jokes! You told me you two were laughing because you were telling knock-knock jokes! But in fact you were laughing because here I was making an ass out of myself pursuing Lew when you'd worked out a whole different scenario for my life! Of all the insufferable, unspeakable acts of arrogance."

She indignantly began wriggling her way out of the sleeping bag, only to be reminded abruptly that she was naked and the sun had long since gone down.

Folding her arms over her breasts, she said through chattering teeth, "Get me my sweater and jeans. I want to go back to The Ladders, and I want to go now."

James burst out laughing. "My dear woman, is that any way to address a Knight of the British Empire? Her Majesty Queen Elizabeth would be highly offended if she could hear you."

"You can take your knighthood and—oh, James, why didn't you tell me?" Her face crumpling up as he gathered her into his arms, she said, "Why did you let me be such an idiot? Why didn't you tell me?"

Brushing back her hair, he covered her face with soft kisses. "Tell you what? That I was Mr. Computer? When it was clear from the moment we met that you think computers and the humanities are at war? You're wrong, by the way, but we'll let that argument wait for another time." Burying his face in her neck, he went on. "Tell you that I'd been tapped on the shoulder at a Buckingham Palace garden party and had a KBE—along with a hell of a lot of other fellows who never could have sat at Arthur's Round Table—when you obviously considered me suspect simply because I'd been able to spring for a raw silk sports coat?"

Sighing, he swirled his hands over her still-shivering body, trying to infuse her flesh with heat.

"I had to tell Didi what you were up to—out of simple humanity," he said. "Beneath that gaudy exterior she's one very insecure woman, and she needed to know that sophisticated, New-York you—that's really how she sees you, so much for her ability to judge character, no, don't hit me, my darling, when I love you so—she needed to know you weren't really going to waltz off into happily-ever-after land with the man she'd fallen for in a big way."

"But you had no right—" she began.

"I had every right. I love you. You love me. And it was pretty obvious that if I didn't take some desperate measures, you were going to defeat me and yourself and doom us to a lifetime apart. And that, my beloved," he said, "was not a tolerable ending to this story."

Another scrap from a magazine article fluttered into her consciousness.

"Jenny . . . You said your ex-wife's name is Jenny.

That's Lady Jenine O'Hara, isn't it," she said in a small voice, remembering from the magazine the face of a flamboyant beauty, dressed in a long paisley skirt and boots, photographed outside an ancient farmhouse. "Did she like sleeping in the musty sleeping bag?"

"You should have read the rest of the magazine article," he said, grinning. "She liked sleeping in or on anything—as long as she had a brand new man next to her. That's what her best seller was all about. *A Thousand and One Knights,* she called it, the clever old darling. But, no, as a matter of fact, we never did share this sleeping bag. The only other person I've ever allowed in here is Phillip, and now that he's old enough for his own sleeping bag, the other half is all yours. If the mustiness doesn't offend you too awfully much."

"Actually, I like it," she whispered. "I'm sorry about your wife. You didn't make it sound as though it had been that awful for you."

"Well, it was partly my fault. My head was always in my machines. I'll never make that mistake again, I can tell you. But maybe the business with Jenny gives you one more clue as to why I fell for you." Holding her close, he said, "Even though it's to my disadvantage, I'm moved by your still feeling loyal to a husband who's been gone for three years. Moved and reassured. But enough's enough, sweet Carrie. It's time for you to say your final good-bye and come with me."

"No . . . no! You're still wrong for me," she burst out. "Wronger than ever!"

His face underwent a lightning change, the tenderness giving way to anger and impatience.

"Why?" he demanded gratingly. "Because it's more than ever obvious how extraordinarily happy we would be? That's the one thing no man is allowed to do, isn't it? Make you happier than Gar made you. But, really, that's not as difficult a proposition as you would like to make out, it is, my Carrie." Taking her face in his hands, fixing her eyes with his, he went on. "Tell me again about his heroic passing."

She squeezed her eyes shut, but she couldn't drown out his voice.

"There was a child . . . He died trying to save a child, you said," James went on mercilessly. "Trying . . . and there was a very strange note in your voice as you uttered that phrase. Did the child make it? Did the child even have a chance?"

"I can't believe you're doing this," she said in an agonized whisper. "Just because Jenny—"

James caught her by the shoulders. "This has nothing to do with Jenny. This has nothing to do with you and me. This has to do with you and only you. Come on, Carrie. Get it out and have done with it forever. He died trying to save a child."

Abruptly, the words broke out of her in a storm of tears and sobs.

"Someone else had already been in the child's

bedroom. Denny Cohn, a great fireman, he was Gar's idol. And he said it was too late, there wasn't any way of getting to the bed, the floor was an inferno; there was no way any child could have survived the smoke. And one of the neighbors was screaming that the boy probably wasn't there anyway; he usually spent weekends at his father's. But Gar went in there and . . . and . . ."

"And—" James prompted, his voice once more replete with tenderness and yet implacably tough.

She grabbed onto his hand and squeezed, and for an anguished moment she remembered her greatest hour with Gar, when she was about to give birth to Dannie and she'd squeezed and squeezed his hand as she'd pushed. And later she'd seen the bruises on his hand, actual black-and-blue bruises, and he'd just laughed and said it was worth it. Yet he'd been willing, almost eager, to give up his life with her and Dannie to make his fatal effort to get to that other child's empty bed.

"It was as if he wanted to commit suicide!" she exploded, finally uttering the agonizing word she'd turned her mind from these past three years. How everyone had conspired with her to keep her from even thinking that word! "The child wasn't there," she went on, her voice high-pitched with relief as she got out the long-suppressed thoughts. "And if he had been in his bed, there was no way on this earth could he have been alive. A hero—oh, yes, Gar was a hero. But he was a coward, too, because he couldn't face the ordinariness of everyday life!"

"Ordinariness!" James's mouth whispered across hers. "How could there be any ordinariness with you? Lord, I'd rather do the laundry with you than visit the Taj Mahal with another woman. Would you and I ever have an ordinary moment, darling?"

"But it wasn't like that for Gar and me. There were lots of ordinary moments. He and I—" Abruptly realizing what she'd said, she tried feverishly to redeem the sentence, but she couldn't for the life of her think where to go. Swallowing hard, she said achingly, "I did mean to make him happy."

"And I bet you did make him happy. Maybe happier than he made you. But some people—you, for shining instance—are happy even when they're miserable, and other people are miserable even when they're happy. Nobody deserves credit or blame for being one way or the other. It's just part of the basic package, like having gray eyes or green."

She pondered his words, moving her head so that she lay against his chest, her ears drinking in his heartbeat.

"You and Jenny?" she asked boldly, after a moment. "You were the one born for happiness, and she wasn't?"

"Oh, yes, indeed."

A peace crept over her, and now she thought surely she would sleep. But she mustn't sleep. If something happened on Dannie's overnight—she wasn't really expecting snakebites, but Dannie might get homesick—she had to be someplace where she could be reached.

"James, dearest? It's absolute bliss being out here with you, but I think we should head back to The Ladders now. Dannie and I have never before been separated for the night, and I don't like the idea that no one knows where I am."

She expected him to protest, but he said he understood.

"No, you wait here," he ordered as she started to emerge from the sleeping bag, only to be racked with shivers yet again. "Papa will provide."

Scampering out into the night, he returned with their clothes.

"The trick," he said matter-of-factly, getting back into the bag, "is to warm each part of the body before putting it into this none-too-warm clothing."

"Won't that make the cold clothing feel even colder?" she asked, her words giving way to a contented moan as he began methodically covering every inch of her left breast with kisses.

"You leave these questions to your man of science," he replied in a muffled voice.

His tongue described narrowing concentric circles around her aureole, turning into a flicking, teasing thing as it reached her nipple. Just when she thought she would have to scream out her longing, he took her nipple in his mouth and pulled at it with his hungry lips.

Her entire body and being seemed to explode

into his mouth as his rhythmic motions created a soaring crescendo.

"James," she called out, her voice cracking. "James. James. James."

As she came back from that world to this, she opened her eyes to behold his grinning face.

"Do you know what just happened?" she gasped, reaching up tenderly.

"I think I do," he said. He jiggled his eyebrows.

"But that's an anatomical impossibility!" she declared.

"I know," he said, calm as anything. "And what do you bet I can make it happen with the other nipple?"

Repeating his sweet, tantalizing motions, he urged her back into a state of wildly heightened desire. And once again all the currents in her body were rerouted, and surging streams of lava seemed to burst forth from her nipple.

Gasping, she stared at him in awe, not quite wanting to believe he had brought her to a level of fulfillment she'd hitherto thought reserved for the most exalted moments of total union.

"And to think that you called *me* a witch," she managed to gasp.

The smug smile was firmly in place. "As the children like to say, it takes one to know one." Slipping her sweater over her head and tenderly inserting her arms into the sleeves, he added, "And now to warm your nether regions."

Before she could protest—but why on earth would she even dream of protesting—his lips drew an imaginary line just below the bottom of her sweater. Spiraling downward, his kisses made every nerve ending in her skin come totally alive, until she was able to register the tiniest shift in the nuances of his motions.

He was warming her—oh, how he was warming her!—yet when he crisscrossed one thigh, then the other, with broad strokes of his tongue, she felt as if she were being clothed less in some practical, protective substance than in a rare gossamer silk. His elegant body floating over her, he then etched radiant lines toward her quivering center, letting her know what sweet torment, what treats, to expect.

At last he was there, at the heart of the matter, telling her with each fabulous movement of his lips and tongue what he wanted her to feel. And what he wanted her to feel was everything!

Impossible, and yet it was happening. She was climbing the mountain again, the mountain was another volcano, and the lava was boiling and bubbling and bursting, rearranging nothing less than the world, and someone was laughing in savage triumph.

"How can you laugh?" she asked through swollen lips only to realize that the laughter had come from herself and not from him.

And now he did laugh, and their lips came together, and on his mouth she tasted a spice that was neither his nor hers but uniquely, wondrously, theirs.

Then he slipped her panties and jeans on, saying, "Let's clothe the bottom half before all my warming-up work is undone."

"Work!" she echoed indignantly.

"As in labor of love."

Reaching for his own clothes, he said, "Do you want to see the coat of arms on my underwear?"

"Stuff and nonsense," she declared. "Knowing you, the only decoration is a hole or two. But I'm sure they're the finest cotton."

He tossed a pair of tattersall modified shorts her way, and said, "You'll have to concede we're pretty well matched in the perception department." He grinned as she took in the Turnbull and Asser label and the one, two, three holes.

"You've got it all in perspective, then?" he asked in evident relief. "The KBE and my business and all?"

She nodded. "I think I do. Even though it threw me at first."

After impudently kissing his shorts, she handed them back to him.

"You know, a man with your physique should show it off," she said. "I can see you in very revealing red bikinis."

"Say you'll marry me, and I'll burn every last pair of shorts. You can replace them with whatever strikes your fancy—bikinis, bloomers, anything."

She watched soberly as he finished getting dressed, and working in silent harmony with him, helped him to roll up the sleeping bag. As they walked back to the car hand in hand, she looked from tree to stone to glistening water, needing to memorize them all.

"You really believe in us, don't you?" she said.

"I do. As I believe in my son, in my work, in the essential goodness of life."

As they started back toward The Ladders, the beam of his headlights picked out eerie tendrils of mist.

"I can't go on saying no to you," she got out, "but I can't say yes. Not yet. Not with the sort of faith you deserve, a faith to match yours. There are still things I'm too uncertain of. The bad chemistry between our children..."

He laughed, but gently. "There's bad chemistry between them the way there's bad chemistry between us. Children are very quick to sense enormity, and to run from it for a while. But all of us together, that's what our children need and crave, and soon enough they'll stop fighting it. And be as happy as they deserve to be." He put a hand on her blue-jeaned thigh. "And will you stop fighting it, Esmerelda? Will you admit that Harold has passed the test?"

"Give me one more day," she said. "To sleep on everything that's happened, and see Dannie, and somehow find a sign that will tell me what I want to know."

He thought for a moment, then said, "Fair enough. Dinner at The Phoenix at eight tomorrow evening— win, lose, or draw?"

"Draw?" she echoed, amused.

"You might decide to be my wife six months out of every year, like Persephone and Hades."

"My favorite Greek myth," she said. "But I absolutely refuse to choose any destiny that requires me to wear a toga."

They cruised along in an easy silence, listening to jazz on the public radio station.

As they pulled into the parking lot at The Ladders, James said, "I hope you forgive me for taking you away from the skinny-dip tonight."

"I forgive you . . . for that."

"But not for being the most wonderful man you've ever met, and loving you madly, and wanting to marry you, and longing to be a father to your daughter?"

"That takes a lot more forgiving, you have to admit," she said, smiling.

As they walked toward Zermatt, he said, "I suppose you know what I'm going to tell you next."

"Yes. That you want to spend the rest of the night with me. And I suppose you know what I'm going to answer."

"Yes," he said. "That you have to be alone."

"I do seem totally incapable of thinking when you're around me," she said.

"That should be grounds enough for marriage right there," he said.

They held each other close and kissed good night.

CHAPTER SEVEN

THE NEXT MORNING, feeling dazed and yet exalted, Carrie put on a fresh pink cotton shirt and a single strand of pearls with her jeans. Glossing her lips to a fare-thee-well, she got ready to meet Dannie's bus—and to face that dazzling enigma, James Luddington.

But when the busful of overnight campers came climbing up from the access road, James was not to be seen among the eager parents. At first Carrie was worried. He was a loving and conscientious father. How could he not be on hand to greet his son unless something dire had detained him? Then she remembered Mrs. Platt. No doubt Phillip's nanny was there among the other unfamiliar folk.

Then, just as the bus doors opened, out popped James from behind a parked van, giving her a wink and a conspiratorial wave. Drawing breath, she realized what he was signaling. She had asked for a day on her own, and he was going to give it to her, by crikey. He would do his best to keep out of her way until their rendezvous that evening at The Phoenix. She was free to stew and search all she liked.

Thoughtful, even delicate, of him—and yet a kind of pressure too. See how wonderful I am, he was saying. See how good I'll be to you.

And would he be good—in a year, or ten years? This man so unnervingly quick to offer his heart and his hand? Or would he need to dance some new dance, solo or with a new partner?

Then Dannie was bounding down the steps, and Carrie was running toward her, thinking of no one else.

"You've gotten bigger! You've gotten older!" she exclaimed, scooping her daughter up. "Did you have a fabulous time?" Hugging Dannie and whirling her before setting her back on her feet, Carrie said, "What do you think about a bath and a quick breakfast at Zermatt before we set off on our next adventure? Oh, where's your sleeping bag, honey?"

"Phillip's carrying it. I cut my finger a teensy bit," Dannie said, proudly holding up a neatly bandaged right index finger, "and Phillip said I shouldn't carry anything."

"He did, did he?" Carrie's mouth was dry as she watched Phillip emerge from the bus, the last one out, clearly slowed down by his down-filled burden. What was it about men named Luddington and sleeping bags anyway?

"Bye, Dannie," a pair of flaxen-braided twin sisters called out as their perfect flaxen mother led them off.

"Hope I see you at the tennis clinic, Dannie," teaching-pro-cum-counselor Bert Magruder said, adding to Carrie, "She was terrific."

Her little girl had done all right for herself on her night away from Mama, Carrie thought proudly. But it was all too clear from the expression on Dannie's happy but grubby face that the most important part of the event had been her changed relationship with Phillip.

As a clearly reluctant James followed his son toward Dannie, the expression on his face seemed to say, I know you're going to make me pay dues for this, but I'm glad our kids discovered each other.

Phillip plumped Dannie's sleeping bag down, then readjusted his own over his shoulder.

"It's all my fault Dannie cut herself," he said, looking earnestly at Carrie through a mist of yellow bangs. "I should have sharpened her hot dog stick for her. But she wanted to sharpen it herself, and I lent her my knife. I guess she doesn't know a lot about outdoor knives, though she's an extremely clever person."

"She is, isn't she?" Carrie returned gravely. "And it's my fault she got cut, in a sense, because I never taught her how to use outdoor knives. And I should have. It's just not the sort of thing you automatically think of teaching a child in New York City, you see."

"Well, when we move to New York I can teach Dannie about knives because she already promised she's going to show me Greenwich Village and teach me how to take the Underground."

Looking everywhere but at James, Carrie said, "I'm glad you two made friends and that you've got some plans for the future. Right now, though, Phillip, Dannie and I have to scoot because we're going off for the day. And I'd like to beat what looks like rain," she added, taking note of the massed thunderheads in the eastern sky.

"I know—to the Alpen Slide. Dannie told me," Phillip piped in his sweet British accent.

At the same time Dannie jumped up and down and said, "Can Phillip and James come with us, Mama? Pretty, pretty please? Because he's in my detective agency now, and everything!"

"Bye, Dannie. See you tonight. Bye, Phillip," Gretchen called with a wave, hopping back onto the bus. The driver was her brother, Dannie explained.

And then Carrie and Dannie and James and Phillip were alone in the parking lot, surrounded by mountains and uncertain sky.

"Because he's absolutely my best friend," Dannie

went on, "except for you and Grandma and Mara. Mom, will you tell James what he has to do so Phillip can go to Hunter in the fall?"

"I will tell James all about Hunter," Carrie promised, congratulating herself on sounding only slightly demented. "But for today, honey—" As she wavered, trying to invent a plausible, forgivable reason for the children not to be together, James came to her rescue . . . sort of.

"You and I are going off on an adventure of our own, old son," James said. "Do you remember the Irish potter you liked so much when you met him in London—Stephen Pearce? His brother Simon blows glass down in a town called Quechee. Furthermore, he's harnessed the power from the dam behind his works to make all the electricity he needs, and that's something I want to see."

"We went there," Dannie excitedly told her new friend. "The glass is as hot as lava."

Blushing because her daughter's innocent words had recalled a not-at-all-innocent grown-up hour, Carrie bent down to retie her perfectly tied sneaker. But James noticed her heightened color anyway, she could tell; of course he noticed.

"Well, I'd rather go on the Alpen Slide," Phillip said, just missing sounding all-American sullen. "You go all the way up to the top of Pico Mountain in a chair lift, then you come down a track on fiberglass sleds, and there are two tracks, actually, a slow one and a fast one. It's a death-defying thrill."

"It sounds as though Dannie was reading you brochures by the moonlight," James answered with an indulgent smile. "I promise you, you shall have your death-defying thrill before the week is out, but I think not today. What do you say, race me back to the chalet? I'll carry your sleeping bag. How's that for being a sport?"

Dannie and Phillip gave each other a last tragic look before their cruel parents separated them, and then, finally, Carrie and Dannie were on their own, and the jangled, heart-tossed, dark-haired mother breathed a sigh of almost-relief.

Almost. An hour later, as Carrie turned onto Route 4 from Route 100, a bathed, fed, and generally restored Dannie said, "This is the same road we took to go to Quechee!"

"Of course. That's how we found out about the Alpen Slide in the first place." But as Carrie gave her matter-of-fact response, she realized she'd had a funny feeling about James's decision to visit the glass blowing operation that day. No doubt he was genuinely interested in hydroelectrical power, but was that his only motivation? Strange, really, that he was being so elaborately cooperative about giving Carrie her day apart, and then chose a destination only a few minutes away from hers!

Glancing into her rearview mirror, she was relieved to see a red Volkswagen Beetle, a blue Saab sedan, a pick-up truck of indeterminate color—and no silver Renault.

"Oh, boy! Oh, boy!" Dannie exclaimed, hanging

out the window as her mother parked the car.

Carrie had to admit the scene merited several exclamation marks. Less dramatically vertical than Sugarbush, yet lusher in its variegated greenness and dotted with a brilliance of wildflowers visible even at a distance, Pico indeed looked almost Alpine.

The open-sided stone building housing the motor that ran the chair lift had been planted about with orange and yellow marigolds and a multitude of yellow-centered white daisies. Round white tables with yellow umbrellas offered a cheerful yet shady place to have a drink.

"Wow! Look at that chair lift!" Dannie said excitedly. "That's better than the Roosevelt Island tram."

"It is, isn't it, honey?" Carrie said, hoping she sounded sincere. She was comfortable with both height and motion, and she knew the chair lift had operated smoothly through many a summer and ski season, yet the sight of the blue chairs, rocking on their wire overhead, most of them empty on this weekday morning, filled her with foreboding.

Or maybe the foreboding had nothing to do with the lift? Maybe she sensed that here on this mountain she would experience a revelation and know once and forever how to answer James.

Maybe it was the weather that was getting to her, she told herself. It was still a schizophrenic sky—sunny in three directions, yet definitely stormy-looking to the south.

"Let's get an all-day ticket, please?" Dannie begged as Carrie approached the stone house.

"I don't know, honey. It looks to me as though it might rain. Let's start with a single ride. We can always come back for more."

"At least get two rides, Mom, please? Because we have to try the slow track and the fast track."

Carrie watched a teenage girl come down on the slow track, knees to her chest as she guided her fiberglass sled down a curving ribbon of cement. Slow looked fast enough for her.

Besides, she needed to stand her ground on some point, on any point; she needed to win one argument with someone, with anyone.

"A ticket at a time," she said firmly. "It costs exactly the same if you buy them one at a time, and that, my darling, is what we are going to do."

As an attendant clanged the safety bar shut over her and Dannie, and their chair began climbing into the sky, Carrie's apprehension seeped away. Really, it was exquisite here. She'd thought of the Alpen Slide as a bit of tourist nonsense, a sly way for the ski-season entrepreneurs to make money even when they weren't making snow, but she had to admit the slide had its merits.

Seen from an aerial perspective, the wildflowers below were flawless specimens—bright as the flowers of fairyland, Dannie was saying. A freshet of water trickled down the mountainside below them, weaving in and out of the flowers, catching the sunlight. Not even the cement tracks could spoil the vista.

Carrie hugged Dannie. "One of the wonderful things about being a parent is that you get to do things like this, did you know that?"

"Of course I knew. When I'm a parent I'm going to come here all the time. And get all-day tickets for me and the kids." But Dannie squeezed her hand indulgently, telling her she wasn't the world's absolutely worst mother.

At the top of the mountain a dark-haired young man in a purple silk warm-up jacket handed them two fiberglass sliding trays and offered them instructions.

"It's real simple. Pull back on the lever to slow yourself down, push forward if you want to speed up. Now, how's that again?" he asked Dannie.

"Pull back on the lever to slow yourself down, push forward if you want to speed up," she recited perfectly.

He did a Fonz-like jig and flipped his pompadour. "Hey, I'm impressed."

"Shouldn't she come down on my sled?" Carrie asked.

"What's the matter, you afraid to go down by yourself?"

Carrie didn't even pretend to laugh, and he hastily added, "She's what, seven?"

"Only six," Dannie said proudly, "but I'm very precocious."

"The kid cracks me up! Believe me, she can handle the sled herself. Five, we tell them to go down with Mommy or Daddy. This kid could handle a 747, right?"

"Right," Dannie said.

None too thrilled at having her parental authority so thoroughly undermined, Carrie crisply picked up her sled.

"Don't forget," the young man said, "if it rains, you stop your sled, get right off the track, and walk down. Nobody here's wearing high heels, right?"

"I read the sign," Carrie said stiffly. Something about the fellow's manner really put her off.

But as she and Dannie were walking past him, he turned the other way to check out the chair lift and Carrie gasped. On the back of the jacket, in gold script, was the word *Oracles!*"

Esmerelda...Harold...the test...the oracle on the mountain! Carrie ordinarily considered herself about as mystical as cottage cheese, but wasn't this an unlikely enough coincidence to put goose bumps on the most resolutely practical of flesh?

"Excuse me—" she began.

He turned around. "Hello, there. Back again? How was your slide? Oh," he went on as Dannie giggled, "you didn't go down yet, huh?"

"What are the Oracles?" Carrie asked. She tried to inject friendliness into her voice. "If that isn't classified information?"

"There's this little-known sport called baseball,"

he began, "and we play it."

Carrie stood there for a moment, disappointed and feeling foolish about her disappointment. Despite the foolish feelings, she hoped he would say more. But what? she chided herself. "Go thou and marry James?" "Go thou and persevere in thy search for a teddy bear?"

Dannie tugged at Carrie's leg. "Come on, Mom. Let's slide!"

And slide they did, down the slow track, Dannie going first so Carrie could keep an eye on her. Once Carrie was convinced Dannie wasn't going to sail off the edge of the earth, and she herself wasn't going to come to a calamitous end, what fun it was! Pulling back on the lever at first, then growing bold and pushing it forward to increase her speed, Carrie exulted in the feeling of freedom. As the wind whipped back her hair and she saw the end of the ride coming all too soon, she realized for the first time in her life why some of her friends would drive six hours to ski for two.

At the bottom of the track she kissed Dannie exuberantly and said, "Let's go on the fast track now."

A delighted grin breaking across her face, Dannie said, "I told you we should buy more than one ticket! Can we get a drink first, though, Mom? Sliding really makes me need Coke."

"Okay, but let's make it snappy. It's looking more and more as though it's going to rain." Indeed, the thunderheads had rolled in closer, and now there were clouds in the west as well.

They had their drinks, but not particularly snappily. The waitress who told Carrie she'd just made a fresh pot of coffee didn't reappear with a cup for a good ten minutes. By the time they were back in the ticket line, Carrie was anxious enough about the weather to ask the man in charge if he didn't think rain was likely.

He craned his neck to check the sky and shook his head. "Nah, you've got a good hour, lady. Maybe two. Now, I'm not going to try to sell you an all-day ticket at this point, but you've got plenty of time to get up and down—even on the slow track," he joked.

Airborne on the chair lift for the second time, Carrie and Dannie tried to identify the various bright blooms below them.

"That's a jack-in-the-pulpit," Carrie said, pointing.

"Where? That purple thing? Oh, yeah. I think they have elves living in them, that's what Mara says. Look, Mom, beautiful dandelions."

Carrie smiled. She supposed that as long as you didn't own a lawn, dandelions were rather beautiful.

When they were halfway up the mountain, suspended high above the ground, they made up names for what they couldn't really see.

"That's a nod-in-the-cradle," Carrie said. "The pink and white striped one."

"And that black and orange spotted one is a pig-soup plant," Dannie said. "It's Phillip's favorite."

The chair stopped.

"Uh-oh, they forgot to pay their electric bill," Carrie said.

"Are you serious?" Dannie asked.

"I absolutely am not." Putting an arm around Dannie's shoulder, she cautiously looked back to see if she could tell what was going on. The man and woman in the chair behind them shrugged in mystification. She turned back.

Dannie swung her feet. "I don't like being stopped."

"Me neither," Carrie said cheerfully. "Nobody does. I'm sure we'll be moving again in a minute."

Dannie looked down into the beautiful ravine below them. "It's about five miles to the ground."

"No, it isn't, honey." Sensing that her daughter was feeling really anxious, she said, "Want to sing?"

Dannie shook her head.

"We could make up our own song," Carrie began.

Instant ballads had gotten them tearlessly through more than a few tense situations. But Dannie shook her head again.

Carrie heard a rumble, and for a lovely moment she thought it was the sound of machinery starting up again. Then she realized it was thunder.

"I wish Daddy were alive." Dannie huddled close to her mother. "Because firemen are really good at rescuing people. Most of the time," she added miserably.

Carrie's temples began to pound, and she suddenly felt herself seized by a rage so fierce she thought it might vibrate her right out of her precarious seat.

You had no right, Gar! she screamed inside her head. You had no right to do this to Dannie, and no right to do it to me, and I hate you, and I'm glad you're dead!

The vile sentiments gave way to a wave of guilt so acute, she thought she would be sick. How could she? Oh, heavens, how could she even begin to think such thoughts?

Sweat poured off her forehead. She'd thought the words she'd said to James during the night had purged her of her unacknowledged pain over the choices Gar had made. Now she realized she'd only just begun to deal with her feelings of having been betrayed.

She turned away, quickly wiping her face with her sleeve, not wanting Dannie to see her distress.

"We'll be just fine, kiddo," she said jauntily, trying to convince both herself and her daughter. "If we don't start up again soon, why, I bet someone like the fire department will come along and rescue us. Isn't this a true adventure? You're going to have fun talking about this to your friends, believe me."

Her heartiness rang horribly false to her own ears, but it seemed to mollify Dannie slightly.

"Well, I just wish my friend Phillip was here, and James. Phillip says James is the smartest man who ever lived. I bet he could make this dumb old chair move." Dannie was still angry, but at least she was no longer so scared.

Carrie put a hand on Dannie's wrist. "Wait a minute, honey. I think someone's trying to tell us something."

Sure enough, the young man in the Oracle jacket was making his way up the ravine below them, broadcasting a message through a bullhorn.

"Ladies and gentlemen, there is no cause for alarm. The chair lift is temporarily out of commission due to a short in the control panel, but we are expecting it to be repaired within the hour. You are in absolutely no danger. Repeat, no danger. We regret the inconvenience. So relax and enjoy the view . . . and thank you again for flying Alpen Airlines. We hope you'll think of us once more should your travel plans bring you to scenic Vermont."

Dannie giggled. "He's a funny guy. I like him." Her moment of panic was over, and she began looking around her with untroubled curiosity.

"Me too," Carrie said with ungrammatical fervor, genuinely grateful for the interjection of humor into that sweaty interlude.

Keeping Dannie calm was one thing, but the reality of the situation was another. An hour! The thunder rumbled again. There was going to be rain in half that time—and very likely lightning too. She tried thinking of every bit of intelligence she'd gleaned as a firefighter's wife, but none of the procedures she churned up were the least bit useful.

There was going to have to be help from the outside to avert disaster, and it was going to have to come soon.

"Wow, did you see that?" Dannie asked as a jagged streak of lightning flashed across the sky.

"Yes—beautiful, wasn't it?" Carrie bit back the desire to scream.

Looking back, she saw the man in the chair behind her making a panicky effort to climb out, and the woman with him frantically pulling him back.

"Oh, Lord," Carrie prayed silently. "Please, please, please, don't let anybody be hurt."

Suddenly, with a glorious, soul-delighting jerk, the chair lift began to move. A glad shout went up and down the line, but Carrie held her breath, afraid to rejoice too soon.

The charm held, though, and after what felt like an eternity, she and Dannie were standing on firm ground.

"Whoopee! Let's go down the fast track," Dannie said.

Carrie didn't know whether to laugh or cry. What extraordinarily resilient creatures children were. How perfectly they intuited the preciousness of each moment of life.

How perfectly one certain man intuited that preciousness too, she thought. One certain man who would never turn his back on this child, or on her, because he knew what love was worth...

"Hurry, up, Mom, before the rain starts."

And there they were, as though disaster had never come close, sailing down the stream of cement.

Into the arms of James and Phillip.

CHAPTER EIGHT

For a moment of searing bliss the four of them were one big beautiful huddle.

Then all sorts of people descended on them, including the Oracle, the ticket seller, and a man in a suit who came racing across from the parking lot. And everybody seemed to want to shake James's hand.

As Carrie looked inquiringly at him, he gave one of his infinitely casual shrugs and put an arm around her shoulders.

"By great good luck we happened to be in the neighborhood," he began diffidently, "and we were

listening to the local news because they were doing
their fund-raising bit on the public radio station instead of playing music, and we heard that the chair
lift at the Alpen Slide was experiencing 'an electrical problem,' and since I have a knack with electricity, I decided to pop over and offer to give them
a hand. And a good thing too," he added as fat
drops of rain began to fall out of the sky and thunder
boomed in the background. "Because the electrician
who was summoned from Rutland has yet to arrive."

The crowd of twenty or so people started moving
toward the shelter of the umbrella-topped tables.

"You mean you saved everybody?" Dannie asked,
openmouthed, plainly thrilled.

"Shhh," James said, hoisting her to his shoulders
in one smooth, effortless-looking move. "Your
mother is suspicious of heroes."

"She is?" Dannie might just have been told that
her mother had been keeping a pet rhinocerous all
these years. "But heroes are wonderful. My father
was a hero."

"Yes, he was," James said gravely, "and that's a
good thing, because every child deserves to have a
hero for a father. And a heroine for a mother."

Phillip looked from his encumbered father to Carrie, who smiled at him. Her heart in her mouth, she
offered him her hand to hold. He took it.

"Mama's the best mother in the entire world,"
Dannie said, "but I don't know if she's exactly a
heroine."

"Oh, but she is," James said. "Because she has the courage to love. And that's the most heroic act of all."

"More heroic than you saving everyone?" Phillip asked.

"Sure. Because when you love someone, you risk getting hurt. How do you feel when I'm mad at you?"

"I hate it." Phillip kicked a pebble.

"Exactly. Because you love me. So you care how I feel about you. If you didn't love me, you probably wouldn't hate my being mad. But if you didn't love me, your life wouldn't be as rich."

"So you and Mama and Phillip and I are all heroes and heroines because we all love people," Dannie said, excitedly bouncing on his shoulders.

"That's right."

"But if Mama's a heroine," Dannie said, "how come she's suspicious of heroes?"

James roared with laughter. "I hope you're considering becoming a lawyer when you grow up."

"Nope. I'm going to be a detective. Or a ballet dancer. Or an English teacher like Mama. Or an electrician like you."

"Excellent choices, all," James managed to say, straight-faced. "And to answer your question about your Mama, I think maybe she's suspicious of heroes because she doesn't really know that she's one of the world's great heroines."

"You mean you didn't know you loved me?"

Dannie wrinkled her nose as she looked at her mother.

"Of course I knew that, sweetie pie," Carrie said. "But I didn't know"—she cleared her throat—"other things. For instance, that I love Phillip. And James."

"Well, how could you know?" Dannie said. "We only just met them. I love them too." Signaling James to put her down, she said, "Come on, Phillip, let's go get the table I had before with my mother. It's got this really gross piece of bubble gum under one chair that I want you to see."

Just then the man in the suit struck a pose and said breathily, "Ladies and gentlemen, on behalf of the management, I would like to invite you all to avail yourself of our refreshment menu—gratis."

"Must be the clever fellow who wrote the copy for The Ladders," James muttered, taking Carrie's hand. "Do you suppose he's also the guy who invented Toga Night?"

They got under the overhang in the refreshment area just before the storm started in earnest.

As the other people scurried for seats, the two of them stood there, locked together, staring out at the descending sheets of rain.

"Are you going to forgive me for rescuing you?" James asked.

Carrie looked at the empty chairs of the lift swaying in the storm.

"I have an important date tonight," she said. "I guess I'm glad I didn't get my hair wet. I forgive you this once. And I thank you," she added seriously, "for talking the way you did to Dannie about her father."

"Someday our children will have to lose some of their illusions. But I don't feel any compelling need to rush the process."

"No," she agreed. She looked over at the table where Dannie and Phillip were giggling together. "Uh-oh—it looks as though they've each ordered a Coke and a ginger ale. But the hell with it. Extra bean sprouts tomorrow. For today, everything's permitted."

"Everything?" Not waiting for an answer, he leaned over and kissed her lingeringly on the lips. "Oh, Carrie. Dear love. I am glad you and Dannie didn't get your hair wet."

Thunder reverberated off the mountain, and she shivered.

The dark-haired young man in the Oracle jacket materialized in front of them.

Holding out his hand to James, he said, "I just want to tell you, I had an idea, and I talked to the manager, and he agreed. We'd like to give you a lifetime pass to the Alpen Slide—and that goes for your wife and the kids."

"I'm honored," James said vigorously. "And perhaps now, with that incentive, the lady will indeed consent to be my wife."

Flipping his pompadour, the Oracle winked at Carrie. "I know it's none of my beeswax," he said, "but I think you should marry him. He's really passed the test."

"What do you say to that, Esmerelda?" James asked as the young man did a little jig and disappeared.

Carrie looked into his twinkling silver eyes. "I say you fed him that line, Harold, when you saw what was written on his jacket."

"Sometimes I think you overestimate me, my love."

She linked arms with him. "Never."

That night, among the lush greenery and cool candlelight of The Phoenix restaurant, Carrie Delaney ate superbly crisped duckling, drank several glasses of a resonant Nuits St. Georges, and presented one withered yet noble scarlet maple leaf to the man she'd found the courage to marry.

Second Chance at Love®

____ 0-425-07773-X	INTRUDER'S KISS #246 Carole Buck	$2.25
____ 0-425-07774-8	LADY BE GOOD #247 Elissa Curry	$2.25
____ 0-425-07775-6	A CLASH OF WILLS #248 Lauren Fox	$2.25
____ 0-425-07776-4	SWEPT AWAY #249 Jacqueline Topaz	$2.25
____ 0-425-07975-9	PAGAN HEART #250 Francine Rivers	$2.25
____ 0-425-07976-7	WORDS OF ENDEARMENT #251 Helen Carter	$2.25
____ 0-425-07977-5	BRIEF ENCOUNTER #252 Aimée Duvall	$2.25
____ 0-425-07978-3	FOREVER EDEN #253 Christa Merlin	$2.25
____ 0-425-07979-1	STARDUST MELODY #254 Mary Haskell	$2.25
____ 0-425-07980-5	HEAVEN TO KISS #255 Charlotte Hines	$2.25
____ 0-425-08014-5	AIN'T MISBEHAVING #256 Jeanne Grant	$2.25
____ 0-425-08015-3	PROMISE ME RAINBOWS #257 Joan Lancaster	$2.25
____ 0-425-08016-1	RITES OF PASSION #258 Jacqueline Topaz	$2.25
____ 0-425-08017-X	ONE IN A MILLION #259 Lee Williams	$2.25
____ 0-425-08018-8	HEART OF GOLD #260 Liz Grady	$2.25
____ 0-425-08019-6	AT LONG LAST LOVE #261 Carole Buck	$2.25
____ 0-425-08150-8	EYE OF THE BEHOLDER #262 Kay Robbins	$2.25
____ 0-425-08151-6	GENTLEMAN AT HEART #263 Elissa Curry	$2.25
____ 0-425-08152-4	BY LOVE POSSESSED #264 Linda Barlow	$2.25
____ 0-425-08153-2	WILDFIRE #265 Kelly Adams	$2.25
____ 0-425-08154-0	PASSION'S DANCE #266 Lauren Fox	$2.25
____ 0-425-08155-9	VENETIAN SUNRISE #267 Kate Nevins	$2.25
____ 0-425-08199-0	THE STEELE TRAP #268 Betsy Osborne	$2.25
____ 0-425-08200-8	LOVE PLAY #269 Carole Buck	$2.25
____ 0-425-08201-6	CAN'T SAY NO #270 Jeanne Grant	$2.25
____ 0-425-08202-4	A LITTLE NIGHT MUSIC #271 Lee Williams	$2.25
____ 0-425-08203-2	A BIT OF DARING #272 Mary Haskell	$2.25
____ 0-425-08204-0	THIEF OF HEARTS #273 Jan Mathews	$2.25
____ 0-425-08284-9	MASTER TOUCH #274 Jasmine Craig	$2.25
____ 0-425-08285-7	NIGHT OF A THOUSAND STARS #275 Petra Diamond	$2.25
____ 0-425-08286-5	UNDERCOVER KISSES #276 Laine Allen	$2.25
____ 0-425-08287-3	MAN TROUBLE #277 Elizabeth Henry	$2.25
____ 0-425-08288-1	SUDDENLY THAT SUMMER #278 Jennifer Rose	$2.25
____ 0-425-08289-X	SWEET ENCHANTMENT #279 Diana Mars	$2.25

Prices may be slightly higher in Canada.

Available at your local bookstore or return this form to:

SECOND CHANCE AT LOVE
Book Mailing Service
P.O. Box 690, Rockville Centre, NY 11571

Please send me the titles checked above. I enclose _____ Include 75¢ for postage and handling if one book is ordered; 25¢ per book for two or more not to exceed $1.75. California, Illinois, New York and Tennessee residents please add sales tax.

NAME _____

ADDRESS _____

CITY _____ STATE/ZIP _____

(allow six weeks for delivery) SK-41b

QUESTIONNAIRE

1. How do you rate _____
(please print TITLE)
- ☐ excellent ☐ good
- ☐ very good ☐ fair ☐ poor

2. How likely are you to purchase another book in this series?
- ☐ definitely would purchase
- ☐ probably would purchase
- ☐ probably would not purchase
- ☐ definitely would not purchase

3. How likely are you to purchase another book by this author?
- ☐ definitely would purchase
- ☐ probably would purchase
- ☐ probably would not purchase
- ☐ definitely would not purchase

4. How does this book compare to books in other contemporary romance lines?
- ☐ much better
- ☐ better
- ☐ about the same
- ☐ not as good
- ☐ definitely not as good

5. Why did you buy this book? (Check as many as apply)
- ☐ I have read other SECOND CHANCE AT LOVE romances
- ☐ friend's recommendation
- ☐ bookseller's recommendation
- ☐ art on the front cover
- ☐ description of the plot on the back cover
- ☐ book review I read
- ☐ other _____
_____
_____

(Continued...)

6. Please list your three favorite contemporary romance lines.

_____
_____
_____

7. Please list your favorite authors of contemporary romance lines.

_____
_____
_____
_____
_____
_____

8. How many SECOND CHANCE AT LOVE romances have you read? _____

9. How many series romances like SECOND CHANCE AT LOVE do you <u>read</u> each month? _____

10. How many series romances like SECOND CHANCE AT LOVE do you <u>buy</u> each month? _____

11. Mind telling your age?
    ☐ under 18
    ☐ 18 to 30
    ☐ 31 to 45
    ☐ over 45

☐ Please check if you'd like to receive our <u>free</u> SECOND CHANCE AT LOVE Newsletter.

We hope you'll share your other ideas about romances with us on an additional sheet and attach it securely to this questionnaire.

• •

Fill in your name and address below:
Name _____
Street Address _____
City _____ State _____ Zip _____

Please return this questionnaire to:
  SECOND CHANCE AT LOVE
  The Berkley Publishing Group
  200 Madison Avenue, New York, New York 10016